"Get out of my van."

"Not happening," Rafe said. Not only was he refusing to listen to Hannah, he was actually starting to smile.

"I won't be responsible for what Fleming's buddies do to you when they see you messing with their boss."

"You're not actually planning to deliver him to his gang, are you? It's hard for me to believe somebody like you would help a known felon break out of jail."

Hannah set her jaw, her hands fisting the wheel. "I have to take him to them as promised or..."

"Or what?"

She chewed on her lower lip. "None of your business. Just go away. I won't tell the authorities which way you went. I promise."

"Suppose I stick around instead, me and my pal, Thor. It looks to us like you need some backup."

Hannah leaned past the dog and made a face at him. "The best way to help is to vanish." It amazed her when he chuckled. "I'm being serious here."

"I'm sure you are, but you're in way over your head, lady."

Valerie Hansen was thirty when she awoke to the presence of the Lord in her life and turned to Jesus. She now lives in a renovated farmhouse on the breathtakingly beautiful Ozark Plateau of Arkansas and is privileged to share her personal faith by telling the stories of her heart for Love Inspired. Life doesn't get much better than that!

Books by Valerie Hansen

Love Inspired Suspense

Undercover Escape

Mountain Country K-9 Unit

Chasing Justice

Pacific Northwest K-9 Unit

Scent of Truth

Rocky Mountain K-9 Unit

Ready to Protect

Emergency Responders

Fatal Threat
Marked for Revenge
On the Run
Christmas Vendetta
Serial Threat

Visit the Author Profile page
at LoveInspired.com for more titles.

Undercover Escape

VALERIE HANSEN

Love Inspired SUSPENSE

INSPIRATIONAL ROMANCE

LOVE INSPIRED®SUSPENSE
INSPIRATIONAL ROMANCE

ISBN-13: 978-1-335-48389-8

Undercover Escape

Love Inspired
22 Adelaide St. West, 41st Floor
Toronto, Ontario M5H 4E3, Canada
www.LoveInspired.com

Printed in U.S.A.

Make no friendship with an angry man;
and with a furious man thou shalt not go:
Lest thou learn his ways, and get a snare to thy soul.
—*Proverbs* 22:24–25

With love to all the relatives and friends who have supported my writing and shared their specialized knowledge to make my books as true to life as possible. I could not have done it without you, my sweet human *Google-ish* minds and hearts.

ONE

Rain pelted the van's windshield. Professional dog trainer Hannah Lassiter shivered. Her stomach knotted. Her hands perspired on the steering wheel and she flexed her fingers. This was the first time she'd actually feared volunteering at the maximum security prison in St. Louis and for good reason. Today it began. There was no way to rationalize the plan she was about to set in motion, not now and probably not ever, yet she had to do it. She had to help Deuce Fleming escape. Her grandmother's life literally depended upon it.

An excited yip from the back of her van reminded her how she'd gotten into this mess. Rehabbing criminals and saving misunderstood dogs had seemed like the ideal way to use her unique skills with canines to serve the Lord and her fellow man. For the last year it had been a pleasant addition to her regular dog training business. But no more. By the time this day was over she, too, would be a wanted fugitive. The thought brought tears to her eyes.

She pulled herself together and feigned calm as she eased to a stop at the gates and rolled her window down a few inches to greet the armed guard. The waning storm gave the air a crisp tang and drops of rain pattered, some breaching the narrow opening. "Morning, John."

"Good morning, Ms. Lassiter." He peered into the van as the canine cargo began a frenzy of barking in response to his voice. "Got a new crop for us?"

"Some likely candidates," Hannah said. She knew better than to try to hurry the amiable guard despite the fact her nerves were firing so fast she could barely control movement and her mouth was too dry to swallow.

"It's a fine thing you're doing," the guard said with a smile. "A fine thing."

Her muttered "Thank you" almost stuck in her throat. "You should get in out of the rain."

He saluted by touching the dripping brim of his cap and backed away.

Fine thing, indeed, Hannah thought. To save her beloved grandma she had no choice but to betray friends and colleagues who had trusted her and sacrifice her successful professional career at the same time. There was no other option, no way to win. In the best-case scenario she would succeed in smuggling a dangerous prisoner out of there without any innocent bystanders getting hurt, including herself. Once she was outside the prison walls and far away from any influence from Deuce Fleming, she prayed she'd find some way to make amends.

After closing the window she proceeded onto the grounds. It was hard to breathe, hard to keep from shaking all over. She was a law-abiding citizen, not the criminal they were trying to make her into. She wanted to help people, not hurt them, and by saving innocent dogs from kill shelters she'd been doing the animals good, too.

Nevertheless, here she was. Caught. Trapped as surely as the guilty men behind bars at the state prison in Lyell, Missouri. They were there for a reason and she was heartsick to have been coerced into helping one of them escape.

Having spent the previous night in prayer, Hannah was positive God understood and would forgive her. It wasn't Him she was going to have to convince of her innocence; it was the new prison warden and the state police. If they failed to see the goodness of her heart and the necessity of today's actions, she was going to end up in big trouble.

"Providing I live through the actual jailbreak," she muttered to herself. By afternoon she would know if the bold plan worked.

Smothering in guilt she sniffled. "And everyone else will know what I've done, too."

Masquerading as convicted killer Rafe McDowell, state trooper Gavin Arthur stayed in character 24/7. This was the toughest undercover assignment he'd ever accepted but he couldn't turn it down. Not when his partner, trooper Andy Fellows, lay in the hospital, fighting for his life after a shootout, and the man's abducted teenage daughter was still missing. Because all clues had led to Deuce Fleming's gang being responsible, here he was, sharing space in prison in the hopes of learning enough to rescue the girl and even the score.

Gavin/Rafe had been briefed well enough to know that Fleming had contacts both inside and outside the prison. Part of his task was to get close to Deuce and learn their identities without revealing that he was the source of that information leak. It wasn't going to be easy. Nothing involving cagey criminals ever was, which explained the need to work undercover. Only two men knew who he really was; his own superintendent and the recently promoted prison warden. Computer files had been created to provide an impressive criminal past and he'd let his beard grow enough to present a scruffy edge. Add to that the tattoos and scars from combat as an army ranger and he appeared to be a damaged, world-worn man who perfectly fit the role.

At present he was sitting in a folding chair in a room with seven other men, Deuce included, waiting for the outsider who was scheduled to teach a dog handling class to selected inmates. While several of the others had brought dogs already being trained and were tending to them, he and Deuce lounged in the chairs as if they had no cares. That, alone, disturbed Rafe. He was aware that Fleming was known as a cool customer but judging by the way the man was behaving, he was more than merely pretending. He truly was at ease.

Rafe crossed one ankle on his knee and folded his arms, making sure his biceps and tattoos were prominently displayed. Fleming met the alpha male challenge in his gaze and returned it with a sneer. "What're you lookin' at?"

Shrugging, Rafe remained nonchalant. "Me? Nothing, man. Just chilling. You got a beef with that?" He saw his quarry open his mouth to reply, then stop when the door swung back. Little wonder. The attractive brunette woman entering the room was impossible to ignore. She was clad in plain denim, boots, and was accompanied by a prison guard escort pushing a cart dolly containing several large kennel boxes and one smaller one. Made of tan plastic, each box had a metal door that was fastened with a small padlock.

Before Rafe could react, Deuce Fleming was on his feet and joining the young woman. He saw her stop dead and flash a tension-riddled smile. The telling reaction was so brief Rafe might have missed it if he hadn't been keeping such a close eye on his quarry. Prison warden Hotchkiss had expressed concern that Fleming had been allowed to join the dog rehab program under his predecessor, but with no proof of dishonesty he'd chosen to let the man continue with the classes. The new warden's goal was to make as few changes as possible to keep from alerting the convict or any of his allies to the undercover officer in their midst. So far, nothing Rafe did or didn't do had seemed to make a difference in Fleming's daily routines or in the behavior of the guards who were suspected of aiding and abetting him.

Rafe leaned forward in his chair and studied the interplay between Fleming and the dog trainer. Although she did her best to hide her feelings, he wasn't fooled. The woman was as nervous as a kitten surrounded by a pack of slavering coyotes. He supposed some of her unease might be due to the place where she was working, but that conclusion didn't fully satisfy. He'd seen enough of her class videos during briefings to know that Hannah Lassiter was normally calm and self-assured while guiding convicts and their assigned dogs through the training process. And she was good at her job. So why the change in demeanor today?

Getting slowly to his feet, Rafe sauntered over to where Fleming was speaking aside to Hannah and offered his right hand to her. "I'm Rafe McDowell. Your new student."

Pausing, poised to be greeted, he was disappointed when the trainer ignored his friendly gesture. Something was definitely wrong. He stepped back several paces to observe her interactions, particularly with Fleming. The con was practically smirking.

Rafe shoved his hands into the pockets of his orange jumpsuit, lounged against the edge of the only table in the room and heard Fleming snort derisively before laughing. The others in the room kept silent as if attempting to keep the peace. A brief glance at the young woman, however, spoke volumes. Her fair skin had paled, her eyes were brimming and there was a tremor in her graceful hands.

Whispering, she said, "I'm ready."

"Shut it," Deuce snapped.

Eyes downcast, Hannah sniffled and swiped at her damp cheeks. Her expression reminded Rafe of a prey animal facing certain capture or death. The poor woman was terrified.

Edging closer by pretending to peer into one of the kennel boxes, Rafe heard the hardened criminal say, "See that you remember your job, Red Riding Hood."

A tear trickled down Hannah's cheek as Rafe made the apparent connection. If Hannah Lassiter was Red Riding Hood, Deuce Fleming was the personification of the Big Bad Wolf and nothing, no one, stood between the two of them but him.

Rafe's main disadvantage, as he saw it, was his place on the side of the criminal element while working undercover. There was no logical way to convince the frightened woman that he was one of the good guys when everything about his persona had been tailored to project the opposite.

Moreover, he reasoned, there was a slight chance the apparently innocent dog trainer was one of Fleming's people. In spite of her uneasiness it was possible she would choose the wrong side if given a chance. He huffed, remembering how close he'd come to making that mistake as a teen and how his friends had rebuffed him after he'd refused to take part in their idea of fun—rampant vandalism and physical violence. Most of them had gone to jail for their crimes.

That memory amused Rafe when he contrasted it to his current assignment. They should see him now.

Hannah could taste acrid remnants of the coffee and toast she'd eaten shortly before heading to class.

Nothing but the threat to someone she dearly loved would have made her agree to the plot she was involved in. The sweet face of her grandmother, Lucy, arose in her memory and nearly broke her. Fleming's cohorts on the outside had been stalking the only remaining member of Hannah's family and had sent her photos to prove it, while nondescript vehicles had been parking outside the house she shared with Gram and were following them everywhere, even to church.

This morning, Gram was safe in the church fellowship hall making lap quilts for a rest home with members of her sewing club, unaware of what might happen later. If Fleming wasn't delivered to a predetermined rendezvous site, his men were supposed to kidnap Gram and hold her until he was free. There was no alternative. No fail-safe plan. It was all or nothing, success or failure.

Silently, fervently, Hannah reached out to God. There were no flowery words to her prayer, no memorized verses, nothing. It was from her heart to the heart of her Savior and so powerful she couldn't help but be strengthened.

She squared her shoulders, pulled leashes from her tote and began to deliver her well-rehearsed opening speech. "Several of you are getting new assignments this morning. I'm going to demonstrate the proper way to handle a dog without hurting it before we work with the new animals I've brought.

Think of them as your canine counterparts. They were jailed and facing execution for simply existing."

"Yeah, they're innocent, like us," Deuce commented, bringing laughter from all the others except Rafe.

"Only one of them has a history of biting and I've been working with him on my own. He was mostly frightened. Back a scared animal into a corner and if he can't run, he'll defend himself in any way he can."

"Humph. I get that, too."

As she bent to unlatch the first of the kennel boxes Hannah whispered, "Understood."

Across the room, Rafe raised his eyebrows and gave the outspoken convict a nod. His task was to get closer to Fleming, not alienate him, so he figured it was best to seem to agree. With the exception of Sam Peabody, an older prisoner who was already handling a smaller dog, everyone in the room deferred to Fleming.

The older man, however, was giving him smug, knowing looks that bothered Rafe. It was as if Sam and Deuce were working together on something.

That put Sam in Rafe's suspect file. Several prison guards were already listed, including the one at the door right now, but other than a few minor incidents in the exercise yard, Deuce hadn't paid undue attention to anyone else. Oh, he had a group of followers. Most cons chose sides for their own protection. But in Fleming's case the men who supported him by their presence weren't forceful types, they were lackeys.

Close observation revealed a tremor in the trainer's hands as she unlatched the largest cage, reached in to clip on a lead and coaxed a dog to step out. It was the largest German shepherd Rafe had ever seen, but its demeanor was that of a whipped cur.

The moment the trainer touched the coarse fur her own shaking ceased and she spoke gently. "It's okay, boy. You're okay. That's it. Take it easy."

Behind her, Deuce snorted derisively. "I

hope you're not planning to give me that coward."

"If you will recall," Hannah said, "the pit bull you worked with the last time was cautious at first, too."

"Yeah, but you said he was just abused. He didn't turn into a sniveling mutt like that one is."

Rafe stepped forward. "I'll take him."

"I make those decisions, Mr…" She consulted the forms the guard had handed her. "Mr. McDowell. But I will keep your request in mind."

Hands spread wide, palms up, Rafe shrugged. "Fine. No sweat." As he observed the quaking canine it occurred to him that the behavior of this dog and the pretty trainer were similar and he wondered if their reasons for fear were also alike. Granted, some individuals were born with a shy nature. That was possible for the dog. But the woman was different. He'd studied videos of her previous classes and if he didn't know it was the same trainer he might wonder if she'd been replaced. Not only was her voice different, so was her body language.

His heart went out to her. Scowling, he watched Deuce posturing and bragging while the other cons stood back. One looked pleased, one frowned, and others did their best to fade into the background as though they were afraid to be noticed.

The trainer caught Rafe's glance and he allowed eye contact to continue for long seconds. Of course she'd be sizing him up because they hadn't met before. That made perfect sense. What was disquieting was the unspoken plea for help he thought he detected in her glance.

Then she bent over the paperwork, made a note in a margin and straightened with the shepherd on his leash at her side. "We will be approaching you, Mr. McDowell. I want you to stand still and avoid looking at Thor. Let him sniff you and don't back away but don't reach for him, either. This introduction has to be on his terms. Understand?"

Rafe nodded. "Yes, ma'am."

He did as Hannah had instructed, and

more. It wasn't hard to feel empathy for the beautiful, shy animal. When he'd accepted this assignment he'd had no idea it would include a dog training class. Being there was the icing on the cake as far as he was concerned. Animals had made his troubled teen years bearable and he'd always had a special affinity for the downtrodden. Or in this case, the literal underdog.

As soon as he got the chance he intended to ask about Thor's history, assuming Hannah knew it. A large male like this one was unlikely to have been attacked by another canine. Chances were, Thor's fear was due to interactions with humans and Rafe intended to show him that not all men were bad.

Hannah had circled Rafe twice, slowly and purposefully, when she said, "You may sit in that chair over there now, Mr. McDowell. Hands in your lap. Still no eye contact."

Instead of turning toward the chair and therefore taking his eyes off Deuce, Rafe backed up. When his knees touched the edge of the seat he sat down. He didn't like the way the outspoken prisoner was leering at Hannah and he sure didn't like the way he was inching toward Thor. A man like Fleming was unpredictable and purposely cruel whenever he thought he could get away with it.

Air in the training room practically crackled with tension. Thor was panting but seemed a bit more relaxed and Hannah was concentrating so fully on the dog she seemed unaware of the increasing human threat. But Rafe knew. His instincts saw more than his eyes could. And he wasn't the only one. The guard at the door had rested the heel of his hand on his holstered gun and the other convicts, even Sam, were inching away.

Hannah and Thor passed in front of Rafe's chair and began to turn to the left. The moment her back was to him, Deuce lunged for her and the German shepherd.

Rafe rocketed off the chair, managed to block the attack with his shoulder and both men hit the floor. What he should have done, he realized belatedly, was provide a distraction rather than go head-to-head with Fleming. Instinct had taken over when he'd put himself between the other man and the apparently innocent woman, leaving him wondering how he was going to spin his actions to appear to be in Fleming's favor.

Strength-wise he knew he could flatten anybody in the room, including the apparently nervous guard if need be. Thoughts of his wounded partner and the man's missing daughter, Kristy, tempered his actions enough to cause him to pull his punches when what he wanted to do was hit hard enough to force a confession. Fleming and his group had already been proven guilty of weapons and drug smuggling. It was only a small step from that to the human trafficking they were now suspected of masterminding.

As far as Rafe was concerned, the only crime worse than that was cold-blooded murder. Nevertheless, he shouted, "Hey, cool it. We're both on the same side here."

TWO

Jumping aside, Hannah barely evaded Fleming's grasp. Thor spun around so fast he tangled her legs in the leather leash and she almost ended up on the hard floor with the grappling convicts.

The remaining kenneled dog barked raucously, joined by the canines in the room, while men cheered the combatants. George, the guard, drew his gun, staying at the door and fumbling for the radio clipped to his shoulder.

Huddled against the farthest wall with Thor, Hannah could barely catch her breath. This was not what was supposed to happen. Not even close. So now what? How could she hope to restore order before more prison guards arrived to disperse her students and ruin any efforts to carry out the escape plan?

Close beside her Thor began to growl. Although Hannah could feel him shaking she had no doubt he was being protective because his posture had changed. His chest was thrust forward as he strained against his collar. A lip began to curl, revealing huge white canine teeth ready for battle.

She wrapped extra leash length around her hand, double grabbed and shouted, "Enough!"

At that moment, Thor barked twice. There was enough menace in the resonating sound to draw everyone's attention, even that of the men wrestling on the floor. They froze. Time seemed to stand still. Hannah didn't relax her hold on the surprisingly protective shepherd, but she did nod to the class. "Chairs. Now. Everybody."

She'd thought about adding a threat to her command before she saw how unnecessary that was going to be. All eyes remained glued to the bristling, snarling German shepherd and the men were moving slowly, deliberately, to obey.

Because she was unaware of Thor's background or previous training, Hannah proceeded with caution. Saying "Good boy" quietly she eased up on the taut leash. The result was positive. Thor stopped snarling and relaxed a little, although his deep growl continued. That was fine with her, especially considering how close her whole class had been to jumping into the two-man melee.

"Fleming, over there," Hannah said, pointing by tilting her head since she still needed both hands on the leash, just in case. "McDowell, to my right. Now."

It was easy to tell the mood of Deuce Fleming. His face was red, nostrils flared, eyes narrowed. In short, he looked ready to tear the other man's head off. McDowell, on the other hand, seemed relieved. He edged in the direction she'd indicated while keeping a table between himself and Fleming. Smart move, she thought, stifling the urge to admire his strategy. An intelligent animal would act the same way because instinct would warn about keeping distance from an enemy.

Distance was exactly what she craved, Hannah reminded herself. But first she had to break the law. That idea was so foreign to her it was making her feel physically ill. Of all the difficult tasks she'd ever faced, this was the worst.

Heart and mind warring with each other, she slowly approached Rafe. There was something about him that instinctively reached out to her. The rest of the room faded into the background when she once again met his gaze.

Normally, Hannah took weeks to decide which dogs belonged with which prisoners, and some never did make the grade, humans or animals. In this instance, however, she sensed something in Rafe McDowell that was missing in the others. The quality that set him apart didn't have a name, nor did it need one. She simply knew he was the right man to work with Thor.

Stopping directly in front of him she laid

a calming hand on the dog's broad head and spoke softly, gently. "It's okay, Thor. This one is okay. See?" She offered her right hand and Rafe shook it.

Although Thor was still trembling he stopped growling. Hannah kept hold of Rafe's hand and drew it closer to the dog's nose so he could sniff it. To her surprise, not only did the shepherd accept the intro-duction, Rafe began to smile. There was a slight sideways movement of Thor's tail, too.

Hannah sighed with relief. "I see I was right."

From across the room, Deuce snorted in derision. Hannah never took her eyes off Rafe, trusting the guard to continue to enforce order. She could see Thor begin to relax more as his new training partner reached forward on his own and made the first touch.

Thor did duck slightly, but he didn't give ground. Rafe sought Hannah's approval with an arch of his eyebrows.

"Yes," she said, "you can keep petting

him. Just be ready to stop if he shows any sign of fear or aggression."

Deuce laughed, "Yeah, man. Go for it. We'd love to see him tear your arm off."

Instead of acknowledging the heckler, Hannah purposefully handed Rafe the leash right in front of the shepherd so there would be no doubt. "He's very intelligent," she said. "He sees that I'm giving him to you. Stand up and accept him, then shorten the slack in the lead to bring him to your left side and tell him to heel."

She didn't know why it surprised her to see Rafe handling the big dog like a pro. Some people had a natural affinity for animals and some didn't. Commands could be taught. Instinct could not. Her greatest fear, besides the planned escape, was that she'd have to leave Thor behind with a stranger. Now that she'd chosen McDowell as his new trainer, a heavy weight lifted from her conscience.

A smaller terrier she'd also brought was soon assigned to a veteran prisoner who had worked with her dogs before, then one by one she let the prisoners demonstrate the commands they had taught their respective resident dogs since her last visit. And, one by one, they were excused to go back to their cells, as usual, until only she, Deuce, Rafe and the guard, were left.

Deuce's demeanor changed once the others were gone. "Get rid of him, too," the convict ordered, gesturing at Rafe as if he was of little concern.

Hannah resisted. "I need to set some ground rules first. He's too new to just be turned loose with Thor."

"What do you care?" Deuce said, sneering. "This is your last day."

Hannah cringed. Shot a quick glance at Rafe. Saw Thor react to the fear she felt and take a step forward. The shortened leash restricted him.

"I thought we were going to keep this just between us," she whispered hoarsely.

"Him?" Deuce laughed and pointedly eyed the prisoner. "I picture this guy getting shot trying to escape. And that useless mutt, too."

"No!" She was adamant. "You promised me nobody would get hurt."

"That was then. This is now. You're the one who let a stranger stick around after I told you to send him away. If anything bad happens it'll be your fault." He addressed the guard. "Are we all set, George?"

"Yeah, but we might need that guy's help lifting the box into her van once you're inside it. That's the only way we'll get you out."

Hannah watched flickers of anger in the convict's expression. Thankfully, he opted to be sensible.

"Fine. We bring him along as far as the loading dock. After that, he's your problem. Got it?"

"It'll be my pleasure to shoot an escaping con," the guard said, smiling. "Now climb into that dog crate and let's get this over with."

As Hannah fastened the lock behind Deuce Fleming and made sure the wire grid of the door was hidden behind the smaller crate; she didn't look at Rafe or Thor. All she could hope for at this point was that he would protect himself and somehow help the innocent dog, too.

It wasn't fair. None of this was fair. She was about to sacrifice her career and maybe her own life because she loved her grandmother, and had been able to see no other way out of the trap Fleming had set for her. She'd made the mistake of mentioning a few personal details in class and the criminals associated with him on the outside were using that information to force her to break the law.

More than once she'd tried to approach the new warden for a private meeting and had been rebuffed. The only conclusion she could come to was that Hotchkiss, too, was part of the broad criminal organization that was working with Fleming. Therefore, she had no choice but to proceed.

Here she was. About to take an irreversible step toward her own destruction. It was like stepping onto railroad tracks, hearing the warning bells and knowing a speeding train was approaching, yet being unable to lift her feet and step aside in time. She was a fatal accident in the making and there was no feasible escape.

Rafe tagged along without being told. He found it difficult to believe Hannah Lassiter was aiding and abetting a criminal even though that was how things looked. If she had shown the slightest affection for Fleming, maybe he could understand it, but she'd seemed to loathe him as well as fear him. So why was she about to smuggle him out of Lyell?

Thor paced Rafe's strides perfectly, never taking his focus off the cart with the plastic kennel boxes and the young woman helping to push from behind it. A second guard offered to help and was rejected, meaning that he was probably one of the honest ones. So far, Rafe's list of insiders was short and until he could get a message to the warden there was nothing he could do to stop the escape other than start shouting about it. Chances were, if he tried that, he'd be the one who was shot and Deuce would still get away in the confusion.

They finally reached a warehouse-looking area and the guard who had guided them there signaled for a cohort to open a garage door. Motors whirred. The door rose revealing the top of a white van level with the floor of the loading dock. Light rain was still falling but it looked as if the deluge was past.

Hannah gasped. "That's no good. Why did you bring it back here? Look at it. We can't load it like that."

Rafe considered making a run for it while the others were distracted, but that would have meant abandoning the woman and letting Fleming get away. The way he saw the situation, his only viable choice was to try to talk his way into the van with the others.

"I can move it," Rafe said. "Or the woman can, if you're not afraid she'll drive off without you."

Fleming made a grumbling noise from inside the box. His orders were muffled but clear enough. "All right. George, keep her with you and let him take care of the van. If he tries anything funny, shoot *her.*"

Rafe took the chance of meeting Hannah's gaze as he said, "I'll just park it off to the side, okay?"

A muttered, "Yeah," came from the box.

At the last instant, Rafe decided to keep Thor with him. He couldn't abandon the dog in the warehouse. If he wasn't presumed dangerous and shot on the spot he'd be hauled off to a shelter somewhere and probably euthanized because there would be no Hannah Lassiter to rescue him. Before the guard could object he was down the concrete stairs, splashing through puddles and climbing into the van with Thor. If the dog had refused to get in, he would have had to force him, but that wasn't a problem. Thor beat him to the seat and moved over to make room as if he'd done it hundreds of times.

Rafe checked the mirrors, inched the van out, backed it into position for ease of loading from the ground and stopped it, engine idling.

By the time he climbed out, George and Hannah were opening the rear doors. They loaded the smaller box without him.

"All right, McDowell," the guard called. "Get over here and give us a hand. We ain't got all day."

"Yeah, yeah." As he rounded the van he prayed that the woman wouldn't notice he'd left Thor in the front seat or say something that might alert the guard. Right now, all he wanted to do was get the crate containing Fleming loaded and secured.

The guard was on the right, Rafe on the left, and Hannah in the rear directing placement. When she was satisfied all was well, she closed the rear doors, then headed for the driver's seat.

Rafe waited, feigning calm while every muscle in his body was screaming for action.

The instant he heard the driver's door slam he tackled the crooked guard hard enough to knock him down, leaped over the prone body and sprinted for the passenger side.

He was half in, half out, when Hannah said, "You're not supposed to be here. Get out!"

"No. Go, go, go," Rafe shouted, gesturing ahead wildly.

Thor gave his face a slurp and moved over to sit on the center console and make room. Momentum of the accelerating van finished slamming the door.

In the side mirror Rafe saw the crooked guard getting to his feet. "Keep going and act natural when we get to the gate," he shouted at Hannah. "George won't dare report my escape. That would stop Fleming, too." He donned a black jacket and ball cap she'd brought along, presumably to disguise Deuce Fleming, then fastened his seatbelt.

She stared at him, incredulous. "You can't do this."

"Looks like I am doing it."

"You're ruining everything. Please, please jump out before we get to the gate."

"Not happening, lady. You heard what they planned to do to me once you were gone."

"They meant it?"

Rafe huffed. "You've got a lot to learn about criminals, Hannah, especially hardcore ones like you're helping to escape. They don't make threats unless they're ready to carry them out."

As he watched, her eyes filled, tears threatening to spill out. She blinked rapidly, then nodded. "That's what I'm afraid of."

THREE

Hannah's fears of what she'd say when they stopped at the prison gate were for nothing. The friendly guard waved her through instead of questioning why she'd managed to pick up a passenger. She felt like screaming. How had this horrible day become so much worse? Even if she was able to explain the coercion behind her initial involvement, there was no way she could hope to excuse helping the second prisoner.

It had occurred to her to find her grandmother, make sure she was safe, then drive to the nearest police station. The trouble was, since Fleming had so many friends inside the prison, what was to say he wasn't just as involved with the local cops on the outside?

Plus, she now had another escapee on her hands. "I'll stop at the next corner and let you out," she told him. The man beside her didn't comment. She slowed, then stopped. "Okay. Get out. Go. Run for it."

"Nope."

"You aren't even supposed to *be* here." Her tone rose. "Get out of my van."

"Not happening," Rafe said. Not only was he refusing to listen to her, he was actually starting to smile.

"I won't be responsible for what Fleming's buddies do to you when they see you messing with their boss."

"You're not actually planning to deliver him to his gang, are you? It's hard for me to believe somebody like you would help a known felon break out of jail."

Hannah set her jaw, her hands fisting the wheel, her neck and shoulders so tense her head was pounding.

"Look, mister, this is not funny. I have to take him to them as promised or…"

"Or what?"

She chewed on her lower lip. "None of your business. Just go away. I won't tell the authorities where I dropped you or which way you went. I promise."

"Suppose I stick around instead, me and my pal, Thor. It looks to us like you need some backup."

"Hah! The dog, maybe. A convict like you, not so much. What was your crime, anyway?"

"Being in the wrong place at the wrong time," Rafe said.

Hannah leaned past Thor and made a face at him. "Listen, you're making a bad situation much worse for me. The best way to help is to vanish." It amazed her when he chuckled so she added, "I'm being serious here."

"I'm sure you are, but you're in way over your head, lady."

A voice from the rear of the van echoed. "Hey, you locked me in. Get back here and open this door."

Hannah saw Rafe arch his eyebrows. Her response was a silent nod of her head.

Rattling and banging and muttered cursing echoed inside the van as Deuce battered the metal grid door of the kennel box. Hannah knew he might spring it open if he continued so she sought to calm him. "Take it easy, Fleming. I told you I'd get you out and I have. Patience, okay?"

"You…"

"Yeah, yeah. You don't impress me with foul language. I've heard all that before."

Thor had begun to growl, obviously sensing her unrest and the mood of the man trapped inside the kennel box. Hannah didn't try to stop the shepherd when he turned a tight circle and made his way to the rear cargo area. While she was driving she could only watch in her rearview mirror but that was enough to see the big dog zero in on the largest crate and put his face close to the metal grid. The effect was immediate silence.

Rafe smiled over at her. "See? I told you we'd be useful."

"And I told you the dog was all I needed. That's still true."

The spread of the man's grin wasn't menacing the way Hannah had assumed it would be. Could he be the answer to her prayers to be rescued from this dilemma? That notion was difficult to accept, yet it was beginning to look like the only possibility around.

She sighed deeply. Gram would sense whether that was true and, remembering past experience, would probably give Rafe the benefit of the doubt. Hannah wasn't ready to be so accepting. Not nearly.

Continuing to drive away from the prison she asked, "What's your story? You never said."

"No, I didn't."

Hannah waited. The only reply she got came from the locked box in the rear of the van. "He's in for murder."

That was not quite the way Rafe would have presented his backstory, but it followed the false criminal record his superiors had set up so he had to go with it. Up to a point.

"I was framed."

Deuce laughed until Thor's single bark silenced him.

"Like the majority of the prison population claims. Care to enlighten me?"

"No, but if I don't I suppose your other passenger will. It all started when I got involved with the wrong people."

"And?"

"And there was a killing nearby. My so-called buddies pinned it on me."

"Ri-i-i-ght." She drew the word out.

Rafe chuckled. "Now you sound like the prosecutor."

"Well, you were convicted."

Crossing his arms he struck a macho pose. "Rotten lawyer."

Her brief chuckle seemed out of place so he studied her. Was she acting or was she actually this functional in the company of one real murderer and a man she believed was also guilty, namely him? Despite his law enforcement training Rafe wasn't sure. It was clear that the pretty dog trainer was nervous. Anybody except a sociopath would be shaken by this untenable situation.

He changed the subject. "Where are we going?"

"A drop-off point. I suggest you leave us before we arrive if you know what's good for you."

"Like I said, I tend to make bad choices. Maybe you're one of them."

"Thanks heaps."

"You're welcome. What happens to you after you turn our passenger over to his friends? Have you given that any thought?"

"Of course."

"So?"

He saw her try to suppress a shiver. "So, it's none of your business."

But it was, wasn't it? Rafe didn't believe for a second that he'd wound up involved in this jailbreak by accident. His desire—his prayer—was always to be given the chance to right wrongs, to be in the right place to benefit someone in need. As far as he could see, this woman needed his help, and more. Unfortunately, as long as she continued to aid and abet Deuce Fleming there was no way he dared reveal his true identity. Therefore, he'd bide his time and roll with the punches, so to speak, although he had high hopes he wouldn't have to risk his life more than he already was.

Yes, he wanted to be a hero. No, he did not want posthumous medals. That was the tightrope he found himself walking. It wasn't a good sign that he found the dog trainer attractive. Poisonous snakes were also beautiful.

Hannah was fighting herself. No matter how much she resisted liking Rafe McDowell, she found her reactions to him warming. There was an unidentifiable quality about him that kept insisting he was a good man. Was it possible that he actually was innocent?

Past experience said, *no.* Her feelings, however, contradicted sensible conclusions. *Am I losing it?* she asked herself. How was it possible to actually begin to like a convicted murderer? Yes, the Bible told believers to forgive everyone, but that didn't mean a person should trust everybody. Discernment had to figure in there somewhere. Statistically, somebody who had taken a life once was more likely to do it again.

Which brought her thoughts right back to Fleming and his friends on the outside. There was no doubt that that man was dangerous. He'd proved it by his past actions and his cohorts had added plenty of emphasis when they'd sent her the jailbreak instructions and those candid photos of her grandmother Lucy's home and habits. They knew exactly who Gram was and how much she meant to Hannah. And they knew how to get what they wanted. She didn't doubt for a second that they would do exactly what they'd threatened if she didn't play along.

Hannah startled when Rafe leaned closer, but since she was driving there was no way to get away from him. When he began to whisper she had to strain to hear his words.

"What happens when he doesn't need you anymore?"

"What?" Her brow furrowed.

"Think about it. You're taking him to his men, right?"

"Yes." Her jaw clenched.

"They won't want anybody to know who they are or where contact was made. What's the easiest way to guarantee that?"

Trying to swallow she found it almost impossible. Her palms were wet, her throat dry and every nerve in her body firing wildly. So much of her concern had focused on Gram she hadn't stopped to consider threats to herself. Would they? Could they? The answer was a flat "*yes.*"

Blinking back tears of frustration she glanced at Rafe. His smile was gone, his dark eyes piercing, his expression grave. Once more he whispered to her. "Why did you let yourself be dragged into this in the first place?"

"It's complicated."

"It would have to be." Easing back into his seat he paused before he asked, "Tell me about your family. Parents? Siblings? A husband, maybe?"

"Just—just my grandmother. She's all I have."

"I see." He crossed his arms again and seemed to be thinking.

Hannah made an abrupt turn and heard cursing from the rear of the van. Deuce Fleming was not a happy camper. But what could she do? How could she save herself and Gram, and while she was at it, an innocent dog and a strangely considerate convict?

"Is your grandmother well?" Rafe asked in a low voice.

"Yes. At least I hope so." Admitting that was akin to a confession and although Hannah regretted saying too much, she was also relieved. Carrying the burden of being the only one aware of the threat had weighed heavily.

"Understood," he said.

Did he really understand? Or was he playing her for a fool, too, same as Fleming had? That was more likely than not.

Too bad she wasn't in a position to be picky about allies.

"Suppose we unloaded early?"

Hannah shook her head. "We can't. I told you it was complicated."

From the rear, Deuce made his displeasure evident again. "Hey. Pull over and unlock this stupid crate. I'm gettin' cramps in my legs."

A quick glance showed the arch of Rafe's eyebrows. "You could drop off your cargo early."

She shook her head. "No. Not happening. I gave him my word. I never lie."

"Humph. What makes you think everybody is as truthful as you are?"

"What choice do I have?" She pressed her lips into a thin line. "And while we're at it, when are you bailing out? I can't have you with me when my delivery is made or they'll think I double-crossed them."

"Who you double-crossing?" Deuce shouted. He began to rock the plastic crate from side to side. Hoping to distract him, Hannah took the next corner fast.

The crate slid across the van, then bumped into the side wall and landed on its side. Thor returned to the front, frightened, and tried to squeeze between Hannah and Rafe. Deuce shouted. "Hey, watch it."

When she looked over to see that Rafe was all right she noticed him concentrating on the side mirror. He turned to her with concern. "Faster. Now."

"Why? What...?"

"We're being followed."

"Are you sure?" Even as she asked it, she knew the answer. The expression on the man's face left no doubt. "Is it the police?"

"I wish." Rafe undid his seatbelt and pushed past Thor to enter the rear of the careening van.

Hannah was frantic. She didn't want anybody to get hurt, not even the cruel man who had threatened her tiny family. Driving erratically was bound to cause injury, perhaps to innocent people. However, if she stopped, whoever was following them could get the upper hand.

"I'm almost to the rendezvous point," she shouted at Rafe.

He had one hand braced on the side of the van, the other reaching toward the huge crate. As she watched, he pushed off the wall and landed atop the crate as if grappling with it.

"What are you doing?" Hannah yelled. "Don't let him out."

"Too late. The door sprang when the crate rolled."

Before she could comment she saw the shadow of a second large male body rising from the floor. Fleming was loose. She'd lost her only advantage.

One of them swung a punch, she couldn't tell which. It connected with a sickening cracking sound. The second man grabbed for the aggressor and they went down again, out of Hannah's sight.

Next to her, Thor had assumed the passenger seat and was watching the fight without making any effort to participate. Hannah supposed that was for the best, given the careening van and the shepherd's lack of professional training.

Wet fallen leaves were piled along the curbs. Hannah wasn't about to slow down enough to give either convict the chance to overpower her so she made the last turn into the parking lot of a strip mall on two wheels, sliding on the leaves and slightly missing the actual entrance. Two of her tires bounced over a curb. The rear doors banged open. One of the combatants was slammed into a side wall and barely missed being ejected.

Hannah saw him make a grab for the other man and miss. She braked hard, hoping momentum would keep either from falling out. It worked for her ally in the black jacket and ball cap. Deuce disappeared through the opening.

Following closely, an SUV swerved to miss the prone body, then slowed to a stop behind her van. Men jumped out both sides and began to gather around Fleming. She could tell they were concerned for him because they ignored the idling van for a few brief moments.

Crawling toward her on the floor, Rafe shouted, "Keep going."

"We didn't kill him, did we?"

"He's still moving, if that's what you mean. Now, drive."

"No. I have to tell them it was an accident. He was fighting and fell out."

"Best thing that could have happened," Rafe countered. He regained the passenger seat, shoving Thor aside to make room.

"Was that Fleming's gang? I need to explain."

"Really?" Rafe ducked as loud booms echoed and glass in the passenger side window shattered.

They were being shot at! She slammed her foot down on the accelerator. Tires screamed seeking traction. Fishtailing, the van slid sideways just in time to head into the drive for the exit and smoothly merge with passing traffic as if she actually knew how to drive defensively.

Seething with anger and trembling all

the way to her core, she covered the next two blocks before she chanced speaking to Rafe. "You've ruined *everything*."

"Hey, I got rid of Fleming for you."

Her fists whitened on the wheel and she could barely breathe when she said, "You may have just killed my Gram."

FOUR

Reaching across, Rafe grabbed for the steering wheel. "Stop the van. We need to talk."

Hannah resisted, going so far as to pound his fingers with her fist. "Let go. You'll wreck us."

Surprised by her resistance he backed off, rubbing his hand. "Okay, okay." Because he'd been watching the road behind he was certain they'd escaped whoever had been following. "Look, I'm just trying to help you out here. Pull yourself together and tell me what's really going on."

"Why should I do that? Why should I trust you?"

That was an excellent question. All he had to do was tell her the truth and she'd know she could trust him, assuming she believed his wild story. Yeah, assuming he also bought hers, he added to himself.

"I could ask you the same thing," Rafe drawled, working to appear calmer than he felt. "You just aided and abetted a prison escape. You're in big trouble."

"Don't I know it."

"Then tell me why." He paused a few beats before adding, "I'm not like Fleming. You know I'm not."

"If I've learned one thing by volunteering at Lyell it's what good liars people can be." She scowled at him for an instant. "Even the ones in uniform."

"Most of the guards are honest."

"And you know that how?"

"Instinct," he explained. "I'm a fair judge of people."

"I wish I could say the same," Hannah countered. She eased the van to the curb and left the engine running. Something in her expression told Rafe that she was close to capitulating so he waited, feigning patience.

When she just sat there staring at him he chanced a slight smile before he said, "Look, you're going to be hunted down by the authorities as soon as they realize Fleming is gone. If I knew more details, I could be a witness that you acted under duress. Get you off with probation, maybe. What have you got to lose?"

"Why would you help me?"

He shrugged. "To even the odds against you? To get back at a lowlife like Fleming? To stick up for a woman who loves dogs and rescues them the way you do? Take your pick."

Hannah's lower lip began to tremble. "I do need help. I just..."

"You just didn't expect to get it from somebody like me, right? Don't make the mistake of waiting for the motorboat when God sends a canoe. They both float."

"God?"

"Sure. You don't think He can show up in a prison? Look at the apostle Paul."

A lopsided grin lifted one corner of her

mouth. "You do a good imitation of a believer."

"Who says I'm faking? Don't you know you're not supposed to judge?"

By this time Hannah was slowly shaking her head, obviously mulling over the apparent change in his persona. Finally, she sagged back in the driver's seat. "Okay. I'm not saying I trust you, but I do need help."

"I'm listening."

"The people who wanted Fleming to escape have been following and photographing my grandmother. They know our every move. I saw the pictures. If I don't show up at the rendezvous point with him when I'm supposed to, they'll kidnap Gram."

"They don't already have her?"

Hannah paled. "I don't think so. I hope not. I mean, she was going to a meeting of her quilting group at church this morning. I phoned her after she got there to make sure she was safe and to tell her I wouldn't be home at the usual time. I didn't want her to go looking for me if I was late. She tends to be overly protective."

"Sounds like you need protecting." Rafe glanced at the clock on the dashboard display. "Would she still be there?"

"Yes. If we hurry. They usually share a potluck lunch after they quilt."

"Okay," Rafe said. "Close the cargo doors and we'll head for the church."

"You could do that for me."

He grinned over at her. "If you're afraid I'll steal your van, pull the keys. I'm not getting out so you can drive away without me. Remember, you're going to need me if kidnappers are waiting for your granny."

"Trust goes both ways," Hannah told him.

Chuckling, Rafe was nodding. "Oh, I trust you, lady. I just know what I might do if I were you. Go secure those back doors and let's get this show on the road."

It didn't surprise him one bit when Hannah fisted the car keys before climbing out. In her shoes he'd have done exactly the same thing.

The sanctuary of the community church had been built of native stone, then added to as different denominations came and went. Sunday School rooms extended one arm of a T and a fellowship hall filled the other with a kitchen at the ell.

The front parking area was deserted, giving Hannah a brief start until she remembered that the ladies usually parked in the rear for ease of access.

"Nobody here?" Rafe asked, leaning forward to peer out.

"In the back, I hope," Hannah replied, proceeding. "Some of them bring portable sewing machines and don't want to have to carry them far."

"Gotcha. Want to stop and let me out here so I can sneak around?"

"And have you desert me when I need you?"

"Hey, that hurts. I told you I'd help."

"Fleming made promises, too. He seemed so nice until he had enough information about my family to threaten us."

"Okay, okay, so you have trust issues. I guess I can see that. How do you intend to explain me to your grandmother?"

"One thing at a time. First, you help me make sure she's safe, then we'll talk about what comes next." She eyed him, hoping he'd be willing to turn himself in when the time came. After all, he hadn't planned to escape any more than she'd meant to include him. Perhaps, told together, their stories would make enough sense to help them both.

The van eased around the corner of the fellowship hall. Few cars remained in the parking lot. A familiar, nondescript green sedan sat at the farthest end of the area. The trunk lid was raised. A slight woman with short sandy-colored hair stood beside it, facing two burly men. Hannah gasped.

"Is that her?"

"Yes!"

Rafe had his seatbelt off and was braced to jump out as soon as the van screeched to a halt. Thor followed in a blur.

Hannah was right behind them. She screamed "Gram" at the top of her lungs.

Before she could come between her grandmother and the men, Rafe's outstretched arm stopped her. Momentarily distracted, she tried to push him aside. When she looked back at Grandma Lucy, the sixty-one-year-old had slammed the trunk lid on the arm of one of the men and was swinging her heavy sewing machine by the handle of its carrying case. It collided with the second man's midsection, doubling him over.

Hannah struggled to free herself from Rafe's grasp while Thor bristled and barked at everybody. "Let me go."

"Hang on," he rasped. "She's got this."

"You have to be…" Wide-eyed, Hannah realized he was right. Lucy was braced like a warrior. She dropped the sewing machine and gave the hunched-over man a karate chop to the back of his neck, whirled and pushed the trunk lid down for the second time, making the first thug howl in pain.

She acknowledged Hannah with a warning look before she grabbed the groaning man by his shirt collar, shoved him toward his partner, then watched as they fled, supporting each other.

A second woman from the church group,

elderly but stalwart, waved a cell phone. "I called the police, dear."

Hannah knew that was the right thing to do in almost every circumstance. This time, however, she wanted time to consult with her worldly wise grandmother and work out the best way to surrender to the authorities. If the police arrived before they had time to talk there was every chance they'd be separated and perhaps forever denied the chance to speak privately.

Lucy joined her with a thankful embrace, then set her away to look into her face. "What are you doing here?"

"I—we—came to rescue you."

"What's going on. And who's *he*?"

"It's a long story. I'm in trouble, Gram. Big trouble."

"Looks like it." She eyed Rafe who was still supporting Hannah by grasping her elbow. "Why's he wearing a prison jumpsuit under that jacket?"

Rafe replied. "Like she said, it's a long story. How about we go someplace quiet to fill you in?"

"Might be worth hearing," Lucy said. "You didn't happen to get a license number of the car those two idiots drove off in, did you?"

Hannah shook her head and blinked back tears, thankful her gram was unhurt but terribly worried about their tenuous situation. Lucy took control, beginning by pointing at the woman with the cell phone. "Go back inside where it's safe, Norma, and keep everybody there until the police arrive." She turned to Hannah. "You two, get in my car and we'll go somewhere quiet to talk this through."

"But, Gram..." Hesitant and more than a little frightened, Hannah eyed Rafe, then Thor.

It was Rafe who complied first, putting Thor into the back seat and holding the front passenger door for Hannah. As soon as she was seated he closed her door and joined the dog.

To Hannah's amazement, Lucy slid behind the wheel as if they were merely friends going for a pleasant Sunday drive.

She'd seen her grandmother stand up for herself before but never physically. And never in such apparently overwhelming circumstances. Now, as Hannah's trembling fingers fumbled the catch to fasten her seatbelt, Gram was acting so calm it was even more unsettling.

If it hadn't been for the escaped convict in the seat behind them Hannah might have questioned Lucy about her hidden expertise. She'd lived with Gram since her teens, but she'd never seen anything like the encounter in the church parking lot. It was as if she'd glimpsed a part of her sweet grandmother she'd never imagined existed.

Boy, was *that* true. The safety belt clicked. Hannah straightened, staring at Lucy. The older woman was smiling.

"Um, Gram?"

Lucy laughed. "I know, I know. You're surprised I was able to defend myself."

"Yeah, a little."

Pointedly glancing in the rearview mirror, Lucy eyed Rafe. "Bear in mind that I'm capable of much more than you just saw,"

she warned. "So don't even think about trying to overpower me to steal my car. Keep
your hands to yourself and mind that dog
or you'll find yourself cuffed and back in
prison so fast it'll make your head swim."

Hannah didn't know what surprised her
more, Gram's threat or Rafe's immediate
"Yes, ma'am."

She swiveled to look at him and her jaw
gaped. He was grinning almost as widely
as Lucy was.

FIVE

Rafe felt as if he'd parachuted into a fractured fairy tale.

Hannah's grandmother was nothing like he'd imagined she'd be, and he was both curious and fascinated. No wonder the pretty dog trainer had been so brave in the face of Fleming's threats. She came from strong stock and a family that functioned well in difficult circumstances. That strength of will was a gift, a trait many people coveted but few possessed. When it was used for good, as in policing or firefighting or other forms of lifesaving, it was a valuable asset. Used the way men like Fleming did, however, it was dangerous.

He decided to plead his case before Hannah explained her part in the escape. "Your granddaughter had been threatened by a guy in the training class. She was told harm would come to you if she didn't help him escape." Seeing the older woman's gray eyes narrowing he raised both hands and quickly added, "No, not me."

"Who?"

"Deuce Fleming. He's…"

"I know who he is. I didn't like it when Hannah told me he was in the class."

"She really didn't have a choice."

"There's always a choice," Lucy countered. "She could have found a way."

"Hey!" Hannah raised her voice. "I'm sitting right here." She made a dour face. "If I'd had the slightest notion you were a martial arts expert I might have resisted more."

Lucy snorted wryly. "Yeah, well, you didn't need to know everything."

"I do now. Where did you learn those moves you used back at the church?"

Sighing, Lucy paused, then explained. "Years ago your grandpa Rob worked for the government. He was worried about being gone on long covert assignments so he taught me some simple self-defense moves. It's been a long time since I practiced but thankfully it all came back to me when I needed it."

Rafe chanced leaning forward slightly to make the conversation more personal. "He'd be proud of you."

"He always told me he was."

The approach of a police car from the opposite direction caused Rafe to duck. When it had passed he resumed his position behind Lucy's right shoulder. "Your family never suspected what your husband did for a living?"

"My daughter and son-in-law, Hannah's parents, knew. They were government agents, too."

A gasp from Hannah was enough to make Lucy reach for her hand. Rafe paused to give them time for silent communication. "What happened to them?" he finally asked.

Before Lucy could answer, Hannah said, "They were killed in an airplane accident when I was sixteen. I've lived with Gram ever since."

The older woman cleared her throat, apparently fighting emotions, before adding her own explanation. "Actually, my daughter was taken—kidnapped—and was being flown out of the country. Her husband lost his life trying to rescue her. Rob blamed himself, of course. I did, too, at first. He'd been trying to break up a human trafficking ring and they'd targeted our daughter in retribution. That brought everything to a head and the brains behind the ring were arrested. The rest died trying to escape with their victims. All aboard were killed when their plane went down in the Rockies."

"Hannah's mother, too?"

"Yes. Missing and presumed dead with the others after the crash," Lucy said sadly.

Hannah stared, eyes wide, lips parted. "You told me Mom and Dad both died in a plane crash, but you never said anything about kidnapping or spies."

"It was the kindest way."

"Kindest?" She withdrew, leaning against the car door as if trying to escape. "How could you keep me in the dark like that?"

"I didn't do it to lie to you—I did it to keep you safe," Lucy insisted. "And speaking of safe, what in the world possessed you to help in a jailbreak? I raised you better than that."

"I did it to keep *you* safe," Hannah shot back. "How was I to know you were some kind of retired spy?"

"My Rob was the actual operative," Lucy countered. "I may have picked up a few tricks along the way, but basically I was just along for the ride." She sobered. "And it cost me my family. You're all I have left. I wanted—I want—to protect you. That's why we have to make this right."

"You just told me everybody I love has lied to me my whole life. Why should I go along with anything you say?"

Rafe decided it was time to chime in. "She may have been less than specific, but she did tell you how they died. My concern is how many guards at Lyell and how

many others on the outside are in Fleming's
pocket. Going to the police right away will
be fine as long as all of them are honest.
Throw one bad one into the mix and anything can happen."

His glance connected with Lucy's in the
mirror. She was nodding. "And you know
this how?"

"Word gets around. Nothing is secret in a
place like Lyell. I was in there long enough
to learn who to trust."

"Is that why you hitchhiked in my granddaughter's van?"

"That was spur-of-the-moment." To his
relief, Hannah provided details of his being
framed for murder, and his narrow escape
from being shot by the crooked guard.

"So, he tricked them?" Lucy asked.

"Yes. I was sure we'd be stopped at the
gate but we sailed right on through."

"Did you? Hmm. Maybe that guard was
in on it, too, and thought you were sneak-
ing Fleming out. Did you consider that?"

"No."

"Meaning he might tell tales about how

you managed to smuggle Deuce past him, probably blame you instead of admitting he was complicit," Lucy ventured.

Hannah's voice cracked. "I can't win."

Rafe and Lucy spoke in near unison. "Yes, you can."

"We'll work this out. Together," Lucy vowed.

Rafe silently agreed. His goal had always been to uncover the people who were backing Fleming's operations, in and out of prison. Putting himself back inside Lyell when his target was free would accomplish nothing. The only drawback to staying with Hannah and her grandmother was that that could put them in jeopardy when and if he caught up with the escaped prisoner.

"You'll need to back off and leave Fleming to me," Rafe said flatly. "Whether the men who picked him up were on his side or not, he's going to blame you for not carrying out his plan to the letter. You need to leave town. Make yourselves scarce until the manhunt is over."

"They'll be after you, too," Hannah said.

He didn't argue. "Forget about me. You two need to stay out of this, period."

The car was slowing as Lucy pulled into the parking lot of a strip mall with a big-box store. "This guy threatened my granddaughter and me. He's also trying to frame her for a felony and ruin the life I swore to guard with every fiber of my being after her parents were killed." She parked and turned off the engine. "What's your stake in all this, mister?"

"Okay." Rafe didn't have to pretend to be disheartened as his shoulders sagged. "Fleming is responsible for the kidnapping of the daughter of a friend of mine."

"Oh, no. Is she still missing?" Hannah swiveled to face him, clearly empathetic.

"Yes. He was shot trying to get her back. It was touch and go for a while. I promised him I'd do everything I could to make things right, even if joining Fleming's gang was what it took."

The closed expression on the older woman's face lent an air of suspicion to her next comment. "So how did you manage to get thrown into the same prison?"

"Friends in high places," Rafe said.

"Convenient. Care to mention names?"

A barely noticeable shake of his head brought an arch to Lucy's eyebrows. She was acting as if she'd guessed which side of the law he was really on while Hannah was still in the dark. Well, fine. Whatever it took to get her to agree to step back was fine with him.

"So," he said, leaning back and giving Thor's head a pat. "It's settled. You understand."

The two women had locked eyes and appeared to be communicating silently. Finally, Lucy nodded and began to smile. "Yes. It's settled. We owe Fleming for what he's put our family through. We're with you a hundred percent."

"Wait, I didn't mean…"

Lucy fisted the car keys and started to get out. Pausing at the door she reached into the center console and took out a small automatic pistol which she passed to Hannah. "I'm going to go buy our new friend some street clothes. If he makes a move, shoot him."

Assuming she was kidding, Rafe started to smile. Then he looked at Hannah's face. The joke was on him. Both the women he'd inadvertently allied himself with had a lot more courage than he'd imagined.

With his back against the rear seat and Thor draped half across his lap, Rafe raised both hands, palms toward Hannah. "Thirty-four long. Shirt XL."

"Shoes?" Lucy asked.

"Elevens. I prefer running shoes." The joke had been inadvertent, but he took advantage of it by adding, "Pun intended."

Hannah wasn't used to holding someone at gunpoint and quickly decided it would be best if she didn't actually point the pistol at Rafe so she lowered it to her lap, aiming away. Instinct told her she was in no danger from this man despite his imposing appearance and evident criminal history. Some of the tattoos on his well-muscled arms had looked more patriotic than menacing and he could have gotten the scar on his cheek and over one eyebrow in an accident rather than during illegal activities. His bearing was different from most convicts, too. Stiff and almost military. Still, she supposed he could have been involved in other activities during his career in lawbreaking.

Sun shone through the window on Hannah's side of the car, warming her shoulders and helping her relax a little. So many questions were whirling in her mind that it was hard to pinpoint what she wanted to ask. Finally, she decided to begin with personal information and made eye contact as an opening gambit.

"You can lower your hands. I don't intend to shoot you. At least not right away."

Rafe gave her a lopsided smile and began to stroke Thor's thick coat. "Thanks. My arms were getting tired."

"Were you telling the truth? Is your friend's daughter still missing?"

He sobered. "Yes. After he was shot, the kidnappers disappeared with the girl."

"How long ago?"

Rafe shrugged and Hannah could see his jaw muscles clenching before he answered. "Seventeen days. We think she's being prepared to be shipped overseas. Since Andy intervened and got himself shot it's been just over two weeks."

"Then she may be long gone."

"Yes. Unfortunately."

"What do the police think?" There was, of course, an underlying reason for asking this question. If Rafe answered the way she hoped he would, she might then be able to unmask his true identity. Assuming he wasn't an actual murderer, she added, hopeful. When he said, "How would I know?" her hopes were dashed.

"I just figured, since you seemed to be connected enough to worm your way into the same prison ward as Deuce Fleming, you must have an inside track."

"It's complicated."

Scowling, she stared at him, trying to peer inside his brain and find the truth. "I don't doubt it. Can't you see it would help if Gram and I knew the details?"

"Help who?"

"Whom," Hannah said, smiling as she delivered the grammar tip.

"Whatever," Rafe countered. "You already know the story of my friend and his daughter. Fleming's people were behind the disappearance. I was there to get closer to him. That's all."

"It's a good thing for you that the former warden was replaced then. He'd have outed you for sure. Hotchkiss actually may be honest, in which case your story might hold water. I'm reserving judgment."

"Have it your way."

"There is one way you could prove it to me."

"How?" Leaning back against the seat, Rafe crossed his arms.

Even beneath the sleeves of the black jacket Hannah couldn't miss noticing how muscular he was. She fingered the gun in her lap, then forced herself to feign calm.

"I could go visit Andy at the hospital and hear the story in his own words."

"Not happening."

"Why not? What are you afraid of?"

"He's still recovering. It might be too much for him to have to relive the trauma."

She humphed. "Or, he might tell me a totally different story."

"Chances are he wouldn't talk to you at all."

"He would if you were with me."

The arch of one of Rafe's eyebrows gave him an intriguing expression. So did the partial smile he seemed to be fighting to subdue. "You actually expect me to take you to my friend's hospital room?"

"Not exactly," Hannah countered, keeping close watch on his face in the hope of catching a clue, however fleeting. "I expect you to take me and Gram."

"Impossible."

"Uh-huh. That's what I thought you'd say, especially if you were lying."

"What I told you about him and his daughter is the truth."

Hannah was enjoying having the upper hand so much she allowed herself to grin. "We'll soon see."

SIX

As Rafe pondered his current dilemma, it was easier to see ways out than it was to envision sticking to the job he knew was his duty. In order to get a handle on the missing teen, he had to locate and interrogate Deuce Fleming, or at least some of his closest cohorts. At present he also felt beholden to Hannah and her grandmother. Once Fleming and his gang got organized enough to plan their next move it was highly likely some or all of them would pursue the women who had thwarted them. Retribution didn't have to make sense when it came to a vendetta. Fleming would be furious, and a man in that state was unpredictable.

An additional reason for keeping Hannah

and Lucy close was for their sakes. Yes, they would be a hindrance. No, he couldn't simply abandon them. Not with Fleming on the loose. If Deuce didn't attempt to get even with them, he'd lose face in front of his gang so he'd have to act. Soon.

Rafe was ready with a plan by the time Lucy returned with clothing for him. To her credit she hadn't shopped for new garments. What he pulled out of the plastic grocery bags was clean but gently worn. The older woman was beyond clever and that was unsettling.

"I'll drive around back of a gas station and you can duck into their restroom to change." She looked pointedly at Rafe. "No tricks. You helped get my granddaughter into this mess and you're going to help me get her out of it."

"No argument from me," Rafe said. "Hannah wants to go to the hospital where my wounded friend is recuperating. I think that may be a good idea. Since his daughter's kidnapping is also tied to Fleming we may be able to learn something that will help us track him down now that he's on the loose."

"Do we need him to prove Hannah is innocent when we have your testimony?"

"Maybe not," Rafe countered. "But if we can take part in putting Deuce back in jail it will count in our favor. As a plus, we might actually get a lead on the missing girl."

"Best-case scenario," Lucy said, pulling into traffic. "It's a bit much to hope for, but nothing is impossible."

Hannah piped up. "I thought you were going to say that nothing is impossible for God."

"Let's leave Him out of this until we see where we stand," Lucy said flatly. "You and I are not exactly dealing with normal people."

Chuckling softly, Rafe sorted through the clothes, amazed at how well the older woman had assembled a casual wardrobe. He smiled. "I'm getting the feeling I haven't joined up with run-of-the-mill folks, either."

A quick glance at Lucy's face in the mirror told him how very right he was. There was a crafty, almost feral look in her gray eyes and they were narrowed at the outer corners as if she was a nanosecond away from a wink. He wasn't going to press her, not right now, but he was getting a strong impression that her late husband, daughter and son-in-law were not the only ones formerly affiliated with a government agency. If sweet old Lucy had not been a covert operator in her younger years, she'd missed a golden opportunity. Everything about her was perfect for the job, including her intelligence and martial arts expertise. She had to have been a master at spy craft to keep her past from Hannah for this long.

And what about Hannah? Rafe asked himself. How deeply was she involved with Fleming. Yes, she looked innocent but that didn't excuse her decision to smuggle him out of the prison. There were other avenues she could have taken instead of breaking the law. Most of the prison staff was honest and he knew from experience that the new warden was beyond reproach. She should have said something to somebody instead of just assuming Fleming was in control.

Lucy pulled to the rear of an older style gas station and stopped, engine idling. "This way you won't have to go through the minimarket part of the store," she said. "Hurry it up. We don't know how much time we have before those yahoos from the church report back with a description of my car."

Wide-eyed, Hannah stared. "Do you think they hung around the neighborhood long enough to watch us leave?"

"I would have," Rafe answered. "If they didn't, they'll know we ditched the van when somebody spots it at the church."

"It's going to create quite a fuss all full of bullet holes like that." Hannah sighed. "I'd just made the last payment."

Checking their surroundings before getting out of the back seat, Rafe jogged to the restroom, relieved to find it unlocked. At least one thing had gone right this morning, he mused. One out of many challenges, unfortunately. Once he was changed and had trashed his orange prison jumpsuit he'd be able to contact his boss without attracting attention. He needed to report in, to try to explain why he'd gone along with Fleming's plan instead of trying to stop him.

A lot of those choices had been dependent upon injury to himself or others in the line of fire, particularly the pretty dog trainer. Ideally, he'd have been able to leave her behind except getting through the prison gates would have been impossible without her and her van. Besides, if he had driven off with Fleming there had been a chance that one of the crooked guards would have blamed Hannah and shot her to save his own skin, just as they'd threatened to do to him and Thor.

No, Rafe decided. To live through the incident they had to be together. Stay together. Work together. It wasn't to his liking or even that sensible, but he couldn't see a way out other than the capture of Deuce Fleming. If he could get himself thrown into the same holding cell maybe he'd be able to worm into the criminal's good graces and complete his original assignment; namely locating the missing teenager.

And in the meantime, he'd keep an eye on a couple of unpredictable and hopefully innocent bystanders. Buckling the belt Lucy had given him, Rafe checked his reflection in the small mirror, put the original cap and black jacket back on and peeked out the exit door. It was only a couple of long strides from there to the corner of the building. If he could slip away long enough to make a call it would sure help his nerves.

He saw Hannah in the car. She was turned around to pet Thor in the back seat. There was no sign of Lucy. Encouraged, Rafe ducked around the corner. No pay phone. He should have known. Common use of cell phones had pretty much done away with the old-fashioned booths.

Almost to the glass doors fronting the service station minimarket, Rafe was caught short, managing to stop just in time to keep from crashing into Lucy.

She grinned at him. "Going someplace?"

"Looking for a snack."

"Uh-huh. I figured. You got money?"

"No."

"I didn't think so. How were you planning to get snacks? Steal them?"

"No. Of course not."

"Keep lying and you'll dig yourself a bigger hole," she warned, gesturing with one hand slipped inside her purse as if she now had the gun. "Get a move on. Back to my car."

"Yes, ma'am."

"And can the politeness, mister. I know you're not what you've told us you are. I just haven't figured out who you really are and which side you're on."

"Ditto," Rafe said solemnly.

Although he'd turned away and started down the sidewalk he heard Lucy mutter, "Good."

As far as Hannah was concerned, everyone was getting along pretty well. She already loved Thor and with Gram in her corner she felt much more hopeful. Rafe, on the other hand, was still an unknown.

The more she learned about him the less confident she became. When they'd parked behind the gas station she'd hoped to have a quiet, intimate conversation with her grandmother and perhaps figure something out. Unfortunately, Gram had bailed out and disappeared around the building as soon as Rafe had closed the door to the men's room.

Seeing them returning to the car together was doubly puzzling and she started asking questions the minute Lucy was behind the wheel. "Will somebody please tell me what's going on?"

"Your buddy here was trying to escape," Lucy offered.

Rafe immediately countered. "I was not. I just wanted a snack, that's all."

"Uh-huh."

There was enough sarcasm in the older woman's tone to tell Hannah she wasn't buying his explanation. She did, however, see his point. "If we're going to drive all over town we probably should stock the car with a few survival items."

Lucy was nodding. "Agreed. We'll stop back at the house and load up."

"The house?" Hannah was scowling over at her. "Fleming's people already know where we live. They've been watching us. We can't go there."

"I have my reasons," Lucy countered.

Worried, Hannah pressed her point. "That's the first place they'll look. We can just stop at a grocery store or something."

Her grandmother's laugh was tinged with enough irony and sarcasm to give Hannah pause. "What? What's so funny?"

"You are. I'm not talking about a bag of chips or a couple of sodas. I'm talking about real survival gear. We can't go into battle empty-handed."

"Hold on. That's not what we're doing." Seeing Gram make eye contact with Rafe in the rearview mirror, Hannah was certain she saw unspoken communication. Talk about unsettling!

Frustrated, she folded her arms and stared straight ahead. "Fine. Have your secrets or whatever. Considering everything I've learned so far this morning, you'll have a hard time surprising me more."

Again, Lucy made eye contact with Rafe, then reached across to pat Hannah's arm. "I doubt that, honey. I really do. I just don't want you to worry."

"Me? Worry? Why in the world would I worry? Huh? I've been shot at and lied to, and I'm currently riding in a car with an escaped convict and a grandmother who's acting like a geriatric James Bond. How would that give me extra concerns?"

"I don't mind being compared to a legendary spy," Lucy said with a smirk. "But I'm hardly over the hill. I thought I'd proved my skills back at the church."

Chastened, Hannah softened and sighed. "Okay, okay. Those were impressive martial arts moves. I—we—were impressed. What I don't like is the way you two keep looking at each other as if you're sharing some big, dark secret. Like it or not, we're in this together. At least tell me enough to give me the tools to help." Surprised at a welling of tears she blinked them back.

"You'll get the gist once I've picked up my gear," Lucy said. "I'm just trying to decide how to explain everything."

"The truth would be a nice start," Hannah said flatly.

"Ah, the truth. So subjective. And so elusive sometimes." Lucy again shot a glance in the mirror. "Right, son?"

Son? Good grief. Now Gram was acting as if Rafe McDowell had been adopted into their family. That was the last straw.

Hannah reached for the steering wheel and clamped a fist around it. "Pull over. Now."

To her surprise, Lucy's resistance was minimal. As the car steered parallel with the curb and came to a stop in the quiet residential neighborhood, she was nodding. To Hannah, she seemed almost relieved.

"Where to start," Lucy murmured.

Although Hannah wanted to answer, she chose silence and let the older woman take her time. Finally, Lucy said, "Okay, honey. Hang on to your hat. You and I are the last survivors of a family of government agents that goes back generations to, long before Roosevelt created the CIA. Their lives weren't as glamorous as the stories about Mata Hari, but they did have their moments."

"Including you?" Rafe asked from the back seat.

"Something tells me you've already figured that out," Lucy said. "I retired long ago but some things can never be forgotten."

"Like hand-to-hand combat?" Hannah asked.

Lucy was shaking her head and pursing her lips. "I was thinking more of the way we lost your mom and dad. That particular human smuggling ring was wiped out, but I can't help feeling as if this situation is giving me a chance to save others from the same horrible fate my own daughter faced."

Gaping at her, Hannah could barely think let alone speak. Rafe, however, did not seem to have that problem. "You'll help me? Really?"

"I just said so, didn't I?"

Beginning to comprehend the connection between Gram's story and Rafe's, Hannah was anything but comforted and she said so. "Count me out. I'm just a civilian with a clean slate. We need to go to the police and turn ourselves in. Closed-circuit cameras at Lyell will prove we were forced to aid Fleming's escape."

Rafe gave a cynical chuckle. "Remind me how you resisted. Did he have a gun on you? Were you accosted on camera?"

"Of course I was."

"Are you sure? Think back. The way I remember it, we worked together to get him into the van and you drove through the guarded gate as if everything was business as usual."

As the escape scenario replayed in her mind, Hannah grew more and more despondent. She had to admit how easy it would be for an impartial judge to view her as guilty. And if some of the law officers who were involved chose to implicate her, she had no proof to the contrary. It was foolish to hope Deuce Fleming or his cohorts would back up her story even if he was recaptured. Still, it would be wrong to break the law again just because she'd been forced to break it before.

"Look," Hannah said flatly, "this is a no-win situation for me."

"Not exactly," Rafe said. "All I ask is that you hold off contacting the police until I've had a chance to reconnect with Deuce and find out where my partner's daughter, Kristy, is being held."

"That's the second or third time you've referred to somebody as your partner. What kind of partnership are you talking about?" Hannah asked.

Above Lucy's laughter in the background, Hannah heard him say, "You'll find out once you meet him so I guess I'd better confess." Of all the things she'd expected he might reveal, the least likely was what he actually said.

"Andy Fellows and I worked together as state troopers."

SEVEN

Rafe figured he could convince Hannah that he was no longer in law enforcement despite his confession so he decided to tell her enough to placate her. The entire truth was not only unnecessary, he knew they'd all be safer in the long run if she didn't expect him to behave like a cop. That was one of the hardest elements of undercover work; bending the law for the right reasons. Someone like Hannah Lassiter, who viewed the world in black-and-white, was bound to have trouble with gray areas. He did, too. Constantly. Keeping focused on the ultimate goal was the only way he was able to keep functioning in such trying circumstances.

Judging by the set of Hannah's jaw and

her scowl, she was not on board the way her grandmother was. That figured for the very reason she'd cited—she was an untrained civilian while he and Lucy understood both sides of the dilemma. It would have suited him better to be proceeding without the pretty dog trainer, but the way he saw it, there was no way to safeguard her unless she stayed close. Undoubtedly, Lucy felt the same.

Rafe leaned over the seat backs to speak to the women in the front, hoping to change the subject. "The best way into the hospital without being noticed is probably through the ER."

"You know what room this guy is in?" Hannah asked.

"I know where he was a week ago so unless they've moved him, yes."

He saw Hannah eye Thor before saying, "I wish I'd thought to grab a *Working Dog in Training* vest out of my van. It's easier to gain access to closed areas when I have a K-9 that's identified that way."

Lucy piped up. "I intend to make that

stop at the house first. You can pick up a spare then."

"No." Rafe was adamant. "That's unsafe."

"For once I do agree with him," Hannah said. "I know for a fact that some of the pictures the Fleming gang showed me were taken there. A couple were snapped through a window. They were that close to us and we had no idea."

"Right now they'll be busy reconnecting with their boss," Lucy countered. "I can't think of a better time to catch them by surprise, get what we need and get away."

Frustrated and upset, Rafe smacked the backs of the front seats with his open hands. "Aargh! You're impossible, lady."

"So my late husband often told me." She was smiling over her shoulder at him. "It never did him much good."

"I gathered. I'm not going to talk you out of this, am I?"

"Not likely. A workman without the right tools is at a disadvantage before he starts."

"Can't argue with that." Rafe was nodding slowly, mentally expanding and altering his plans. Since the escape everything had been in flux anyway so he'd have to remain flexible, even if it meant listening to this civilian.

"Hey!" Hannah interjected. "Don't I get a vote?"

Rafe's "No" was echoed by the older woman.

"This is not a democracy," Lucy added. "I'm calling the shots."

Rafe almost laughed aloud when Hannah made a face and said, "I suppose it's too late to vote you out of office or arrange a coup."

Chuckling quietly, Lucy said, "Honey, it was too late the minute you came to live with me. I promised God I'd always look after you and I intend to keep that promise. Period."

Hannah huffed. "You sure have a funny way of showing it."

"Not at all," Rafe said, looking to Lucy to be certain she understood what he was trying to tell Hannah. "Calm down and think this through. Your Gram and I have experience and skills that you don't. It's nothing against you, it's simply a fact. If you're half as smart as I think you are, you'll listen to us and let us make the important decisions."

"Put my life in the hands of two people who are such great liars that I was totally fooled? That doesn't sound like a good idea to me."

Sobering, he pushed away and sank back into the rear seat. "Good or not, that's how it is."

Fuming and struggling to accept the night-and-day difference in her grandmother, Hannah barely took notice of their surroundings until Gram missed the turn into their familiar driveway. Hannah's head whipped around, her gaze pinned on their house as they pulled farther and farther away. "Hey. I thought we were going home."

"We are."

"But you just passed…"

Lucy's hands were fisted on the steering wheel, her concentration as much to the rear as forward. "Something was off. I don't know what it was, but my instincts have always been good. We'll go around the block and get a fresh look."

Hannah flinched as Rafe leaned forward again and asked, "What am I looking for? What did you notice?"

"I'm not sure. Call it a subconscious warning. I know better than to ignore it."

"Terrific." Hannah straightened in the bucket seat and faced forward, trying to process the nightmare her life had become in the space of a few hours. She supposed it was normal for her to resist accepting such a drastic change in Gram but this was bordering on lunacy.

Finally, she formed coherent enough thoughts to express them. "Look, you guys, we've lived in that house for years. I know what it looks like and I didn't see anything odd when we drove by, okay? Let's just grab whatever we need and get out of this neighborhood before Fleming's men figure out we're here."

Instead of arguing with her, Gram gave

a slight nod and kept driving. "The black SUV down that side street. Did you see it?"

"Who, me?" Hannah asked.

"No," Lucy said, "I was talking to our friend in the back seat."

"Yes," Rafe replied. "And the old pickup in a driveway right behind it, too. Could be either, or both."

Listening, Hannah felt so left out she was ready to scream, or cry, perhaps in unison. "Stop it. Just stop it. You're scaring me."

As if he, too, was anxious, Thor laid his big head on her shoulder. She could feel the canine trembling and felt responsible for some of his angst. Sensitive animals picked up on human emotions as well as those of their own species, and she'd probably been sending out waves of fear despite the outward calm she was trying so desperately to project.

Hannah laid her cheek against the side of Thor's muzzle, cupped his face and consciously slowed her breathing. She might not understand people as well as she liked, but it was easy for her to connect with the spirits of animals. Maybe that was because words weren't necessary, although a softly spoken "good boy" could have a beneficial effect on almost any canine.

As a child she'd missed her parents when they'd had to be away for work, which finally made sense now that she knew their secret occupations. Before they had been killed in the plane crash, they'd relocated the family every couple of years and Hannah had repeatedly been the outcast, the new kid in school, so she'd made friends with animals, particularly dogs, to fill the void. In retrospect, she could see the plus side of that choice and it comforted her slightly.

Glancing over at Gram, Hannah felt a deep sense of loss, not of her actual grandmother but of the person she'd thought her grandma was; the safe homebody who had taken her in as a teen and finally given her stability and security. The one who had loved and accepted her wholly, without reservation.

And the one who had lied to her from the

beginning, she added, blinking back tears. She could understand the subterfuge when she'd been an impressionable teen but she was a mature adult now. If these compli-cated circumstances had not warranted a confession, would Gram ever have told her the truth?

What else was she still holding back? Hannah wondered. Finding out that she'd been raised in a family that was all pretense had been bad enough. Was there more? Was Lucy continuing to pretend or was what Hannah was seeing now her real persona? Did someone who had lived a double life have the capacity to revert to the kind of unvarnished truth normal people took for granted?

Hannah would have asked that question aloud if Lucy hadn't abruptly pulled into a long, narrow dirt driveway and stopped at the end. "Where are we? What are you doing?"

"Remember when you were little and used to come visit me and Grandpa? We let you play in the wooded lot behind the house, but the old cabin back there was always padlocked."

"Right."

"Well, there was a good reason." Lucy climbed out. "This is it. Follow me."

"What about Thor?" Not knowing what lay ahead or how long they'd be away from the car, Hannah was concerned for the dog.

"Leash him and bring him. We won't be coming back."

"What? I thought we were here to pick up supplies."

"We are," Lucy said. "And to ditch my car."

Although she was proceeding to let the big dog out, Hannah felt trapped in a bad dream, one that kept getting creepier and creepier. Reality had morphed into a hazy scenario that melded childhood memories with the solid reality of a nondescript little wooden building that had sat, undisturbed, in the wooded plot for as long as Hannah could remember. Surely, that couldn't be where Gram had stored survival equipment. It didn't look big enough for more than a couple of backpacks and maybe a folding cot.

Keeping Thor on a short leash was not only sensible under the circumstances, his proximity gave Hannah a feeling of security and boy, did she need it. One of her companions was her beloved grandmother who was not the benevolent person she'd been pretending to be. The other was either a hardened criminal she'd met in the prison or an undercover cop who did such an amazing job of faking his anti-social persona he'd been able to convince prisoners and guards alike. So which was he? And what was she going to do with the older woman who had been playing the part of a normal run-of-the-mill senior citizen?

Hannah was more than confused, she was disappointed and disheartened. Nothing was as she'd thought and nothing would ever be the same again, not now that she knew the truth about her family. Part of her wanted to be proud of their patriotism. A more personal take on the situation had her feeling so bereft she didn't want anything to do with anybody, particularly the two people she presently found herself stuck with.

Halting abruptly as they approached the small cabin, Hannah kept Thor close at heel. Lucy, in the lead, didn't seem to notice the change but Rafe did. He approached closer and reached out. His hand almost touched her shoulder when the dog began to growl and bare his teeth.

Rafe froze, speaking quietly. "Lucy. We have a situation."

The spry, older woman paused and looked back. "What's wrong?"

"I suspect your granddaughter is about to rebel."

"I wondered what took her so long." She smiled. "Hannah, honey, I know this is a lot to take in but you need to trust me. We can get out of this in one piece if we work together, and that means following my lead."

"I don't even know who you are anymore." Her narrowed gaze shifted to Rafe. "And you. You're probably as bad as Deuce

Fleming. Maybe worse, since you're apparently playing both sides against each other."

"I told you, I'm one of the good guys."

"Right." Hannah's voice was rising. "And Gram told me she was a regular grandmother living out her golden years after retiring from her job as a county clerk. I don't know who to believe but one thing I am sure of—I'm not getting in any deeper than I am already. I don't have to protect Gram anymore and I sure don't have to defend you." She set her jaw and tried to keep from sounding hysterical. "I quit. Here and now. I know where I am. You two can go off on whatever idiotic mission you think is necessary. I'm going to walk out of these woods with my dog, turn myself in to the police and explain everything."

"No, you are not," Rafe said. The underlying menace in his tone gave Hannah the shivers. She looked to Lucy, expecting moral support, and was shocked to see her shaking her head.

"Gram?"

"You need to do this our way to have

the greatest chance of survival," Lucy said. "I don't trust your friend here any farther than I could throw him, but we need him as backup and to give us a connection to Fleming, providing we're able to locate him under amiable circumstances."

"Why go looking for trouble?" Hannah was starting to show panic.

"Because an organization like Fleming's isn't going to just leave us alone after what's happened. They'll have to punish you to save face and believe me, it won't be a slap on the wrist. If you were anybody else's granddaughter I'd recommend witness protection but even that isn't foolproof. No matter how careful the US Marshals Service is, a good percentage of people with new identities are eventually located and eliminated. This isn't a kid's game we're playing, Hannah. This is life and death. There are no do-overs. The minute you agreed to take part in the jailbreak, you were permanently committed."

"They said they were going to kidnap and kill you if I didn't cooperate."

Lucy pulled Hannah into a motherly embrace and gently patted her back. "That's partly my fault for not telling you the truth long ago. If you'd known my real history, you might have come to me with your problems instead of getting sucked in by a clever crook."

"He had pictures of you," Hannah reiterated. "Lots of them. He showed them to me on a phone somebody had smuggled into prison."

"Meaning he had people on the inside, like your friend here claimed," Lucy reminded her. "That's another reason we have to give this guy the benefit of the doubt."

A branch broke in the distance. Thor growled. Hannah jumped. Lucy thrust her away and deftly inserted a key into the padlock that secured the cabin door. She stepped back out of the way and gestured. "Everybody inside. Now."

"But…"

Hannah found herself being swept up and half carried through the open doorway by

Rafe. Lucy was right behind them while Thor circled at the end of his leash.

A shout echoed. Another answered. Hannah was struck speechless by confusion and raw fear. What she still wanted to do was turn herself in, but it was looking as though that was no longer an option. Whoever was outside the cabin was approaching, and judging by the noise they were making they weren't very concerned about being spotted or reported.

That made sense. Nobody else would know where they were unless Gram used her cell phone to call for help and chances of that happening were slim.

Thoughts whirling, Hannah belatedly realized she'd left her own purse behind in the van when they'd switched cars. She didn't have her phone and had no identification with her. The only defense she had left was the novice K-9. And her own wits.

Rafe turned to slide a heavy timber across the weak-looking door to bar it. Hannah stood motionless in the center of the fifteen by fifteen cabin, unsure what, if anything, she could do to help Lucy.

That question was answered in seconds. Lucy lifted a tarp, levered open a trap door and pointed. "Go."

"I can't. We can't." Hannah pulled Thor closer. "He hasn't learned to climb ladders."

"I'm not leaving you behind," Lucy said, clearly determined.

Rafe stepped up. "Help me sling him over my shoulders. I'll carry him down."

Hannah's loud *"No"* blended with her grandmother's. Voices outside were growing louder. Something solid hit the cabin door so hard it jarred the whole building and knocked dust from the low rafters.

The men outside attacked the wooden door again and again until the air inside the cabin was clouded with swirling particles of dirt. Hannah coughed.

Rafe stripped off his jacket and thrust it at her. "A sling. Make the dog a sling. And hurry!"

Her hands were shaking so badly he had

to help her tie the arms together behind the dog's shoulders. "Keep tension on the leash," he shouted. "Here we go."

EIGHT

Lying prone, Rafe fisted the knotted arms of the jacket and began to lower the dog through the trap door. At this point he half expected the frightened animal to snap at him but Thor made the short drop easily. Lucy was at the bottom to catch him and Hannah scrambled down next.

"Pull that door in after you," Lucy ordered Rafe. "Make sure it latches in place and push that rod through the U-bolts."

As he did as he was told, he wondered what possible advantage there was to locking themselves in a subterranean chamber with potential assassins waiting for them above. It didn't take long for him to realize he'd been underestimating the older woman. Not only was she opening the door to an underground passage, she looked pleased with herself.

He huffed. "I don't believe it."

That made Lucy smile. "Believe it, mister." She started down the dark narrow corridor, patting the walls as she went. "Keep up and I'll have us out of this in a jiffy."

"This is why you didn't want me to play in the shack?" Hannah asked softly.

"Among other things. It needed to look unused. Derelict. We didn't want anybody else messing with it, either. It took forever to set this up ."

"Where does this passageway lead?" Rafe asked.

"My house. Once we enter the basement, stealth will be crucial. I assume all of Fleming's men followed us into the woods, but they may have been smart enough to leave someone behind. If that's the case, we can't take a chance on him sounding an alarm."

Rafe knew what she was implying and hoped it didn't come to a confrontation under these circumstances. As far as Deuce Fleming knew, Rafe was a fellow escapee.

To catch him in the company of Hannah and her grandmother would cast him in a different light, particularly if he couldn't convince the gang that he was keeping the women with him as hostages.

He reached out to tap Lucy's shoulder. "I have a proposal for you."

"No time for making deals, mister," she said.

A keypad lit up under her touch and she punched in a series of numbers. Rafe tried to see them over her shoulder and failed, not that there was any proof he'd need the combination to that lock again, anyway.

Lucy began to ease open the door into the cellar. A musty odor assailed him. Hannah seemed to be more at ease now that she was about to enter familiar space and, consequently, Thor was more settled, too. To Rafe's relief the ambient light from high windows showed a normal staircase as an exit.

The only audible breathing came from the panting canine. Hannah had him on a short leash and was tiptoeing along behind her grandmother. There were no sounds from the house above and apparently nobody close by outside, either.

Falling back, Rafe gave them plenty of space while he cast around for a makeshift weapon. The retired secret agent was undoubtedly armed with the gun from her car and Hannah had the dog to protect her, meaning he was the only one walking into who-knows-what empty-handed. That hindrance he intended to remedy ASAP.

He was reaching for a heavy wrench atop a tool bench when Lucy glanced back. Rafe froze. Was she going to ditch him here and now because she didn't want him armed? He raised both hands, palms facing toward her. "I just want to be able to defend myself."

"Second drawer down, far left," Lucy said in a hoarse whisper, "and keep it quiet."

Cautiously, Rafe followed her instructions. The drawer contained a tangle of fishing line, old lures and floats and plastic packets of snelled hooks. He pushed them aside and spotted a long narrow sheath. A fish filleting knife.

He picked it up and displayed it, waiting for Lucy's acknowledgement. At her nod he threaded the leather sheath through his belt. Any worry he'd had about whether or not she trusted him was negated.

The shocked expression on Hannah's face, however, gave him pause. She looked as if she was trying to decide if she should conk him with the nearest shovel or scream and make a run for it. To her credit, she did neither.

The three humans and one dog gathered at the top of the interior stairs. Lucy eased open the door and peered out. Rafe held his breath. Then she was through and moving quickly past the kitchen and down a hallway with Hannah right behind her.

The women and Thor turned into a bedroom. Rafe decided to post himself at the door as their rear guard. His back was to the wall, his palm resting on the hilt of the knife. Every sense was heightened.

Braced to repel an attack, he waited.

* * *

Hannah wished she had a chance to sit down and mull over everything that had occurred since breakfast. Not that she wasn't capable of thinking on her feet. Until today she'd congratulated herself on her decisiveness and quick thinking, and now it occurred to her that much of that pride was misplaced. Then again, she'd never have imagined finding herself in a situation like the one she was experiencing. People were proving that her reserved personality was one of her best traits because the more interaction she had with her companions, not to mention the thugs pursuing them, the more she yearned to withdraw, to nurture the shy, reclusive person she was before and to make everybody else vanish along with her troubles.

That, of course, was not going to happen, at least not until something else changed. Sadly, she remembered little about her parents other than the fact that they were away often and she'd stayed with her grandparents during those times.

Trying to picture her mother and failing to produce a clear memory, Hannah gave up and looked to Lucy. Not only had the older woman disappeared into the bedroom closet, she was tossing things out onto the carpeted floor.

One black backpack landed with a clunking sound. Lucy straightened and pointed at it. "Pad that with extra clothing so it doesn't rattle."

"Mine or yours?"

"Go get some of yours from your room," Lucy said. "Warm clothes and shirts you can layer if the weather changes. I can handle this by myself. And take your dog with you."

What Hannah really wanted to do was pitch a temper tantrum and refuse to aid anything illegal. That reasoning almost made her laugh aloud. Since her actions at the prison had started all this, she figured she owed the others at least a modicum of cooperation, particularly with erstwhile assassins prowling around the premises.

Startled to find a man standing like a

statue right outside the bedroom door, Hannah started to swing the heavy pack at him, then recognized Rafe just in time to stop. Her heart was threatening to burst out of her chest. At her side, Thor panted happily, tail wagging.

She faced Rafe. "What are you trying to do, scare me to death?"

"Nope. Watching your backs."

"Did Gram tell you to do that?"

"No, my training did. We need to operate as if there is danger around every corner, which may very well be true. I suggest you save your indignation for a better time and start thinking the way your grandmother and I do. It'll keep you alive longer."

"God gave me life and He will look after me, especially if I keep His commandments."

"I agree, to a point," Rafe said. "He also allows us to make our own mistakes and with those errors in judgment come consequences. Being a Christian doesn't mean we'll never have trials, never be disappointed. It means we won't have to face them alone."

"Right now," Hannah said, making a face at him, "I'd settle for all the alone time I could get."

"Away from people, maybe. Don't turn your back on your faith. Please."

"What makes you think I'd ever do that?"

"It happens, okay. I almost made that mistake when Andy's daughter was kidnapped and he was shot. I asked plenty of questions, but in the end I chose to trust the Lord enough to agree to go undercover at Lyell."

"That whole story is true? For real?"

"For real."

Reading unspoken confirmation in his dark eyes, Hannah was finally able to believe him. Relief flowed through her as if she'd been locked in a prison of her mind and had suddenly been released.

She sighed noisily. "Okay. One thing at a time." She held up the pack. "Gram wants me to pad this with some of my clothes so it doesn't make noise."

"Where are they?"

Hannah pointed. "Over there. We only have two bedrooms."

"Do you always close the doors when you leave?"

"No, I..." Scowling, Hannah did a double take. "No. We usually leave the interior doors open." Before she finished her sentence, Rafe had withdrawn the filet knife, pushed her aside and was approaching the closed bedroom.

"Thor would have alerted me if there was anybody in there," she said.

"Humor me."

Moments before, she would have argued. Something had changed. It was subtle enough to miss had she not been so tuned in to the situation. To him. Viewing him through new eyes she let herself appreciate his courage as well as the way he looked with that dark, wavy hair and expressive brown eyes.

The first time she'd met him, in the prison, she'd made a personal assessment that was now being expanded at light speed. Rafe

McDowell had been ruggedly handsome in the training class, yet she'd refused to admire him as a man, choosing to classify him on the level of her arch nemesis, Deuce Fleming. Now she was seeing a handsome, concerned, wildly brave hero who was risking his life to save others, including her. That viewpoint made all the difference.

A blush warmed her cheeks. Thor had been way ahead of her in assessing Rafe's character, hadn't he? The enormous shepherd had sensed the good man beneath the hardened persona and had accepted him within minutes of their meeting. As a professional dog trainer she knew she should have heeded the animal's instincts then and there. Perhaps in the deep recesses of her brain she had, at least enough to bring him to meet Gram.

Was that why she'd given in and had taken him with her to the church? Hannah wondered. Had she been fooling herself about Rafe to keep from liking him even a little?

Watching him ease open the door and step

through, Hannah felt a surge of warmth, of concern, that merely added to her appreciation of the man.

Aloud, she whispered, "Be careful." In her mind she prayed, "Jesus, help us all."

Rafe moved out of sight. There was a crack, then a thud.

The door swung in and a shadowy figure emerged, fleeing.

Thor broke away from Hannah and barreled down the hallway chasing someone dressed all in black. Out of sight, a door slammed so hard it shook the window panes.

Hannah entered the bedroom in time to see Rafe levering himself up off the floor. When he stood, however, he was clearly lacking balance.

"I took a swipe at him. Might have caught his arm. I'm not sure." Staggering, he lunged toward the doorway and caught himself with one hand on the jamb. "Which way did he go?"

"Thor chased him off." Hannah proceeded to grab clothing and stuff it into the pack.

"We have to stop him before he alerts the others."

"Too late for that," Hannah said, relieved to see the K-9 returning, tail wagging, tongue lolling. "Looks like the guy got away." She dropped to one knee and hugged the big dog's thick neck ruff, checking for hidden injuries as she said, "You were wonderful."

Rafe's "Just doing my job" struck her as terribly funny, and although she tried to keep from giggling, she failed. Once she started it was impossible to stop. Soon, she was laughing so hysterically it drew Lucy over at a run.

She knelt beside Hannah and Thor. "What is it? What happened?"

Wiping away tears and struggling to catch her breath, Hannah finally gestured toward Rafe and managed to explain, "When I said 'you were wonderful,' I was talking to the dog."

NINE

Rafe insisted, "I knew that," but both women were enjoying laughing at his expense so much that neither seemed to hear. Rather than belabor the point he checked his head, feeling the rising lump, and was relieved there was no bleeding.

"If either of you care, one of the gang conked me, but I'm okay," he said.

Lucy regained her composure first, sniffling and wiping her face with her hands. "Good to hear."

"That guy ran off, thanks to the dog. I think we'd better get a move on."

"When you're right, you're right," Lucy said. She pointed at Hannah who was still chortling and brushing away tears. "Let's get this show on the road."

"How? We left your car in the woods."

"We left one car in the woods. Who says that's all I have?"

Rafe slipped his arm around Hannah's shoulders to guide her through the door and also to temporarily prop himself up. His head was clearing quickly but he didn't want to slow their escape. At the last second he remembered the backpack and grabbed it by one of the shoulder straps.

"You hid a whole car for an emergency?" he asked.

"Of course not. That would be overkill. I just never sold my late husband's wheels. There's a pristine Dodge Charger under a tarp in the garage."

Picturing the sporty car, Rafe arched a brow, discovered that it made his head injury hurt more and schooled his features. "I assume it will hold three."

"Four," Hannah said, ducking out from under Rafe's arm and tugging on Thor's leash to keep him close.

If the older woman hadn't been grinning when she turned to look at him he would have worried when she said, "If we're short on room, we can stuff the felon in the trunk."

"As long as you don't try to put Thor in there," Hannah quipped back, also smiling.

Rafe was starting to wonder what kind of unstable family he'd gotten himself involved with until he recalled the common stress relief habit of many first responders after a particularly difficult assignment. They called it gallows humor, the darkly funny comments that not only helped them release tension but also distracted their wounded minds from the reality they dealt with on an almost daily basis. He wasn't particularly surprised to hear Lucy resorting to such wry humor, but he was a bit unsettled when Hannah joined in so effortlessly.

"I'll hold the beast on my lap if I need to," Rafe said, joining the spirit of the conversation. "At least *he* likes me."

Ahead, Lucy held up a hand, signaling a stop before easing open the side exit off the kitchen. Rafe saw her listening intently, as was he. The house and garage seemed deserted except for their little party. Nevertheless, he saw Lucy draw her gun, signal once more, then step down into the darkness.

The irrational urge to accompany her hit Rafe. He knew the woman was a pro and on her own turf so she'd be safer than anywhere else, yet he still wanted to cover her back. That was part of his training, of course, and the reason why partners were so important. They could be the difference between life and death.

Thoughts of poor Andy and his missing teenage daughter dumped Rafe's mood lower than the cellar they'd used to escape. It wasn't just a job for him. Not anymore. It was penance. A calling beyond anything else. He'd failed Andy and his daughter, Kristy, and he intended to make things right again, one way or another.

His problem now was the added responsibility for two civilians who were anything but normal, and who had ended up swimming in the same pool of hungry sharks where he was trapped. In retrospect he couldn't see any way he could have changed previous circumstances to avoid the mess they were in, yet he kept thinking, wondering, imagining a different scenario.

If he'd been positive the women would be safe in police custody he'd have told them to turn themselves in. Unfortunately, he wasn't convinced that that was the best course of action. Truth to tell, he didn't know what was.

Lucy reappeared out of the dimness, startling Hannah enough to make her jump and leading Rafe to grasp her shoulders. When she didn't object he kept hold for extra seconds before releasing her.

"You," Lucy said, pointing to him, "Go back to the room I was in and bring the two duffle bags I left on the floor. I'll have the trunk open for you to stow them."

"Then what?"

"Then you get in as fast as you can. Drag your feet and we'll leave you behind. Got that?"

"Affirmative," Rafe said, slipping into official jargon. He wanted to ask for her assurance she wasn't planning to ditch him regardless but thought better of it. She could have chosen plenty of other ways to get rid of him if she'd wanted to, yet she'd not only kept him with them, she'd provided a weapon.

He moved swiftly and stealthily through the silent home, located the bags she'd readied and returned with them. A shiny black Charger sat in the rear of the garage, waiting. An overhead door began to rise. Rafe expected the car's powerful motor to roar as soon as he'd loaded the trunk and slammed the lid. Instead, he heard the starter turning over repeatedly, as if the battery was not quite powerful enough to start the engine.

Holding his breath as he dove through the door into the rear seat he sent up a silent prayer for success. Once the car was running its generator would recharge the battery. The key was that first cough, that first catch after being left idle for so long.

Lucy tried again, rested a moment, then turned the key once more. The car sputtered, then roared. She raced the engine. Black smoke billowed from the rear.

Looking back over the trunk lid, Rafe saw movement. People? Yes! "Goose it!" he shouted, realizing that Lucy was already doing just that. Tires squealed as they spun and slipped on the cement floor.

As the Charger fishtailed out of the garage and straightened in the long driveway, the rear window shattered into a thousand tiny shards.

Rafe grabbed Thor without thinking and pushed him down in the seat to protect them both.

Even a low growl was not enough to cause him to let go.

From the front he heard Hannah shout, "Down," and felt the K-9 drop below him. Before he had a chance to thank her she was climbing over the center console into the back seat with him and the dog.

"I'll take care of him," Hannah shouted. "Get up front with Gram where you can help her."

It occurred to Rafe to ask how he could

hope to help while they were fleeing in a speeding car. Instead, he obeyed. His long legs gave him trouble but he managed to finally get squared away and slide down into the bucket seat.

There was no doubt that Lucy was a master at defensive driving. He was thankful for that since they seemed to have eluded the assassins.

"How can I help?" Rafe was nearly yelling.

"Center console," Lucy shot back. "In the bottom."

Lifting the lid and reaching deep, Rafe felt the hard, cold metal of another gun. "You want me to…?"

"Yes. I can't very well drive and shoot at the same time." Inclining her head she indicated the rear seat. "Hannah is a crack shot, but I'm not sure she's up to firing at a human target."

"And you think I am?"

"I know you are," the older woman said. "I saw it in your eyes before you said a word to me back at the church."

He saw no reason to argue. She was right. As much as he loathed the idea of harming anyone he was trained to make that decision when he must. It was nothing to be proud of. It was simply a fact. Sometimes even those sworn to uphold the law had to employ deadly force in the course of their duties.

After removing the firearm from the console he examined it, extracted the clip to make sure it was fully loaded, then reassembled the gun and cocked it. "Ready."

"I figured you would be," Lucy said, grimacing. "You're not my first choice for a partner but you'll have to do."

Remembering his mistaken reply to Hannah back at the house, Rafe smiled wryly. "I should be your first choice. Don't forget. Hannah says I'm wonderful."

From the back seat came a loud, clear, "Hah!"

As far as Hannah was concerned it was no longer necessary to visit the wounded state trooper in the hospital to prove Rafe's backstory. However, since Gram was driving and had practically deputized him by giving him a gun, she figured she might as well go with the flow, so to speak.

Once they had reached busier streets in downtown St. Louis Lucy had begun to drive more normally. Hannah's nerves insisted she keep watching the traffic behind them, to no avail. They weren't being followed. Best of all, whoever had been on their tail would have no idea where they were headed or when they'd surface next so they couldn't be setting up an ambush.

Thoughts like those reminded Hannah of the predictable plots of old Western movies. Too bad she couldn't rewind reality the way you could a video recording.

Intent on soothing the frightened shepherd, she stroked his fur while staring out the car windows. Cold air was whooshing in through the broken rear glass, making her glad she'd grabbed a hoodie as part of her getaway wardrobe. As soon as they stopped she planned to fish it out of the pack. In the meantime, she warmed herself by cuddling Thor.

In the front seat, Rafe was pivoting to keep scanning their surroundings. Hannah met his gaze when it landed on her. "What?"

"Nothing." Smiling, he turned away. "I'm just glad your furry pal didn't bite me when I shoved him down to keep him from getting shot."

"I think he's decided you're one of the good guys."

"What about you?" Rafe asked. "Have you decided that, too."

"The jury's still out, but I have to say you've been consistent. And if Gram trusts you, I guess I do, too."

"You don't make up your own mind about things like that?"

"I used to," Hannah said, "before I made a big mistake and got too friendly with the men in my prison class."

"Not everybody is like Deuce Fleming," Rafe reminded her.

Lucy had been staying out of their conversation until then. "Enough are to make me leery. In this case, however, I'm glad it's all turning out this way. I've waited years to even the score for my family."

"Vengeance is Mine, I will repay," Hannah quoted from scripture referring to God's promises.

Lucy snorted a wry chuckle. "True, true. I do believe the Good Lord evens the score eventually. The thing is, what's to say He isn't doing it through us this time?"

That seemed right and wrong at the same time. Hannah held her peace until Rafe piped up with a heartfelt "Amen." Then she shook her head and said, "I think you're both wrong. I think this is happening as a result of what I've done."

"Plenty of guilt to go around," Lucy said wisely.

Catching Rafe's eye in the side mirror Hannah was convinced she saw signs of his sorrowful agreement. Perhaps this was a good time to quiz him regarding his former law enforcement partner.

"Tell me more about this man we're going

to see at the hospital," Hannah urged. "I don't want to say the wrong thing and make him worry more. What set this whole thing off, anyway? An assignment or pure chance?"

Noting the squaring of his shoulders she didn't ask more. As he finally began to explain she was glad she hadn't. The situation was worse than she'd imagined, meaning Rafe and Gram had been right taking the unfolding of events so seriously.

"Andy and I were part of a task force looking into the disappearances of high school– and college-aged young people. We were getting close to unmasking the gang behind the kidnappings when Deuce Fleming was arrested for parole violations and sent back to prison. He was incarcerated when Andy's daughter, Kristy, was taken so it was evident he was running the whole show from behind bars."

"Okay. That explains why you were undercover, but how did Andy get hurt?"

"He thought he had a hot tip about a warehouse that might be Kristy's location.

We requested backup before going in but his fatherly urges were too strong to wait. I should have stopped him from making entry. Instead, I went with him."

"And he was shot."

"Yes. We never saw the sniper. Clearly, we'd been set up and fell for the oldest trick in the book."

"No Kristy?"

"No Kristy or any other teens, either. The place had been used as a halfway station at one time, but there was no current activity and very few clues."

"What's the connection between what happened and Fleming? I'm not seeing that clearly." Hannah paused. "I mean, how can you be sure *that* gang is the one that took Andy's girl?"

Rafe cleared his throat as if there was a huge lump in it before he explained further. "Because they taunted our team. We had word Kristy Fellows was missing hours before she was reported gone from school. They not only took her, they were proud of doing it."

"So you went to prison."

"Yes. It was the least I could do under the circumstances."

"It was dangerous."

Rafe huffed. "Everything I do on the job is life-threatening. Being in prison was just one more way to die. Like you said before, if it isn't my time it isn't my time."

"Except that God allows us to make mistakes, as we all know. There can be extenuating circumstances."

"Agreed," Rafe said. "All I can do, all any of us can do, is our best in any given situation."

"You've got that right," Lucy chimed in. She was slowing for a turn into the hospital parking lot so Hannah sat back.

Had she ruined Rafe's chances of rescuing the teenager? Hannah asked herself. *Please, Lord, no.* The unspoken plea was followed by a more specific prayer. *Father, let me make this right and not mess it up again. Please, please.*

There was no booming voice from heaven, no flash of divine lightning to let her know she'd been heard, yet she was sure she had. Courage and trust in her faith would play a big part in her future actions, of course, and there was always Thor to rely on, even if no people stayed by her side through this trial.

Yes, she wished she'd had more time in which to assess and train him. He'd clearly had some lessons in walking on a leash and defending his handler against attack because she'd seen that in action. Reliably calling him off was another story.

Nevertheless, Hannah thought as she slipped an arm over the shepherd's shoulders and gave him a pat, he was large and formidable-looking enough to make an actual command for pursuit and takedown unnecessary. She hoped. Smiling slightly, Hannah corrected that thought. It was more than hope, it was assurance. Her actions for the greater good would be blessed. They had to be. The alternative was simply unacceptable.

TEN

"I think Hannah should stay in the car," Rafe told Lucy as she parked.

As expected, the dog trainer had other ideas. "No way."

He shook his head. "Your grandmother and I can do this without you and the dog. You can't leave him locked in the car alone. He'll get scared. You should stay with him."

"I intend to stay with him," Hannah shot back. "All the way to Andy's room and back."

"Security won't let him in." At least Rafe hoped not.

"They will once I put a training vest on him. Gram, pop the trunk and let me grab my hoodie and the special harness."

"I take it I'm outnumbered," he muttered as he straightened beside the car to tuck the gun into the back of his belt.

Lucy huffed and smiled while Hannah dressed herself and Thor, then faced Rafe, hands on her hips. "You betcha."

"That's what I was afraid of." Turning, he led the way toward the side entrance portico. Unless someone in the hospital intervened and stopped them he was going to have to put up with his unwanted entourage. Well, so be it. He'd dealt with plenty of uncomfortable situations in the past. Compared to most of them, this was not so bad. What bothered him most was providing adequate protection for them all while they were out in public. Risking his own life was one thing. Letting civilians do the same was entirely different.

Except for signs warning of contagion and portable sanitation stations, the small lobby leading to the emergency room was essentially empty. Someone pushing a patient in a wheelchair passed them as they entered the double swinging doors, and he could see nurses ducking in and out of Emergency room cubicles but that was all.

"Third floor, rear," he said, ushering the

others to an elevator and pushing the call button. Panting, Thor was seated politely on Hannah's left. Lucy flanked her on the right. The older woman was obviously well trained and aware of the chances they were all taking. That helped Rafe relax a bit. So did the obedience of the K-9. He'd liked that dog the minute he'd laid eyes on him and nothing had happened since to change his mind.

Crossing the threshold into the elevator was new to Thor. He cringed and stopped. Hannah's gentle encouragement brought him through and once inside he seemed calmer, although Rafe could see him trembling.

"I told you to leave him in the car," he said.

"He'll be fine," she countered. "This would be part of his regular orientation, anyway."

"I guess getting shot at would be too, right?"

"I hope you mean like what happened

when we were in the car. You haven't seen any threats here, have you?"

"I'd have told you if I had."

Lucy agreed. "So would I."

Everyone fell back behind Rafe as he led the way onto the third floor and headed for Andy's room. The so-called patient in the second bed was actually an armed officer. The task force had chosen to protect their injured member that way to avoid making a guard evident. In truth, the powers that be were using Andy as bait, hoping Fleming's gang would try to finish the job and leave themselves open to capture in the process. Secrecy was paramount, meaning Rafe was not about to inform his present companions. Not unless he absolutely had to.

He pushed open the door. Andy was sitting up in bed, eating with the hand not hampered by a sling. The second bed had privacy curtains drawn around it.

Grinning, Rafe greeted him. "Good to see you looking so well, buddy." As he spoke he cast a telling glance toward the other bed, wondering why the officer sent to guard Andy hadn't stopped them. "Everything okay?"

Andy pushed away the tray table and scowled at Rafe, then looked past him at the women and dog. "Yeah, yeah. What's going on? Why did you abandon your assignment?"

"I didn't." Approaching the bed he gestured. "This is Hannah Lassiter, the dog trainer from Lyell. Fleming coerced her into helping him escape. I went along to keep an eye on him."

"So, where is he?"

Shrugging, Rafe shook his head. "We don't know. We believe that members of his gang have him and are taking his orders because they've been trying to get even with us for botching his escape. We should be able to get a line on him soon." He paused. "Providing they don't kill us first."

"That's a comforting plan. Is that the best you can do?"

"For the present," Rafe said. "Hannah and Lucy, her grandmother here, have a target on their backs so we're sticking together in this. I brought them to see you to prove I'm on the up-and-up. We've all had to do things we didn't like and it's my goal to get back in Fleming's good graces as soon as possible."

"By hanging out with them?" There was barely disguised anger in the wounded man's words.

Rafe understood. "It just worked out this way, buddy. Once they were involved I couldn't abandon them. Deuce would have killed them in a heartbeat."

"What about Kristy?" Andy was almost shouting. "What about my daughter?"

"I'm not giving up," Rafe promised. "Lucy has experience with human trafficking operations and may actually be of help to us."

"And the dog lady?"

"She's the reason Deuce escaped, yes, but she wants to make amends, and Thor has already been useful."

"I take it Thor is the dog and you're not

hiding a Viking bodybuilder out in the hall."

"Right." He chanced a smile. "We will do this. I promise we will. I'm not sure why I ended up saddled with this posse but here we are."

From behind him Rafe heard Hannah's indignant "Hey…" before Lucy silenced her with "Hush."

Seated between the women, Thor stood and began to growl. Rafe tensed. Looked to Hannah. "What's wrong with him?"

"The mood in this room is probably affecting him." She laid a hand on the shepherd's broad head. His whole body had started to shake worse than it had in the elevator.

Rafe drew the gun Lucy had given him and stood with his back to Andy's bed. Thor was still growling and staring at the closed-off area containing the second bed.

"Give him some slack," Rafe told her. "Just enough to tell us what he senses."

Andy piped up. "It's probably the guy in the other bed. He's okay."

"Do you know his name?"

"Brad, something."

"Okay, Brad," Rafe said. "Hands in the air and open the curtains."

Long seconds passed. Rafe tensed more when he saw Lucy draw her own gun and push Hannah to the side. Thor resisted, remaining focused on who or what was behind the heavy privacy curtains.

A shot echoed in the small room, skimmed over Andy's bed and left a round hole in the window.

Hannah shrieked and ducked to protect her K-9. Lucy took a two-handed shooter's stance. Rafe jerked back the curtain. "Freeze. Police."

A black-clad figure bolted out the opposite side and through the exit.

"Are you all okay?" Rafe shouted, hesitating momentarily to check for himself.

Satisfied at the answers, he yelled, "Hold the dog," ran for the door and burst into the hallway, aiming at the ceiling for safety. Except for a nurse standing there, frozen in shock, it was empty.

* * *

Gripping Thor's leash with both hands Hannah was barely able to keep him from giving chase. Control by the handler was essential, of course, particularly since neither she nor Rafe knew what the dog might do inside a busy hospital. Moreover, if Thor was triggered by the sight of a running man, he might go after Rafe, himself, instead of the man he was chasing.

She watched her grandmother begin to relax, then move to check on Andy as soon as Rafe reentered the room. Instead of going to his former partner, however, he swept back the curtains to reveal the empty bed. Correction. It wasn't empty. There was a young-looking man lying in it, moaning.

"Is that Brad?" she asked, hardly needing an answer.

Andy confirmed it with a nod. "Is he okay?"

"I think so." Rafe pushed a call button to summon a nurse, although Hannah figured they'd have plenty of company in the room soon, thanks to the gunshot.

"Did the shooter get away?" Again, an unnecessary question. Making eye contact with Rafe Hannah said, "We can probably use Thor to track him if we hurry. Otherwise, we'll be stuck here explaining to Security who we are and why we came."

Wheeling, he grabbed her elbow and called to Lucy. "She's right. Let's go."

There was no way for Hannah to command Thor to track since she hadn't trained him yet so she simply let him lead her out of the room and down the hallway. He stopped at the elevator they'd used to get there. Whether that meant the shooter had left that way or the dog was merely retracing his own steps was anybody's guess.

The door slid open immediately. Thor leaped over the threshold and Hannah followed.

"Is this how he got away?" Rafe asked her.

"It may be. Or the dog may just want to leave. It's impossible to tell until we get back to the lobby or parking lot and see which way he goes from there."

"Better than nothing," Lucy said flatly, pushing the door close control, then ground floor. "I wasn't looking forward to explaining how we got these guns into the hospital and why we need to keep them."

"Yeah."

Hannah could tell Rafe was upset, probably more at himself than anyone else, although she supposed there was enough disappointment to go around. He'd made a tactical error by not checking the other bed space himself rather than just taking Andy's word for it. Desire to be in and out of the hospital as quickly as possible did explain it, although she figured poor Rafe had to be beating himself up over the lapse in judgment.

Thor pushed his way past Lucy and Rafe to lead Hannah out of the elevator. Because he immediately turned toward the main exit she assumed he was merely taking her back to the parking lot.

She ordered him to stop at the curb outside by giving the leash an abrupt tug. "Sit."

Rafe joined her on the side opposite the

canine while Lucy flanked her on the other. Sirens in the distance were getting louder fast. Feeling his hand at her elbow again Hannah looked up at him. "You could leave me and Gram here and take her car."

"Not unless you have a death wish," he countered. "Whoever was up there with Andy now knows for sure that we're working together. That blows my chances to convince Deuce I was acting on his behalf when I went with you."

"I hadn't thought of that." Hannah peered over at Lucy. "Is he right?"

"We'd have to make a lot of assumptions to be sure. Probably."

"So, now what?"

"We find a safe place to talk it over and regroup," Rafe said.

Letting the leash slacken, Hannah was surprised to have Thor pull to the side. "Hold on. Our car is over there." She pointed. "He wants to go the other way. Maybe he is actually tracking and doesn't know how to tell us."

"Okay," Rafe said. "As long as we get

away from the building we should be okay for a few more minutes. They'll have us on camera and once they check their videos we'll be IDed."

"How long?" Hannah asked.

"If they're efficient, maybe ten minutes. We can't count on any longer."

"All right." Hannah stepped off the curb and began to follow Thor's lead. He put his nose to the ground a few times, apparently relying mostly on airborne scents. There was no wavering, no hesitation to his mission and she was beyond thrilled. This K-9 was even more special than she'd thought when she'd pulled him from the shelter in spite of a sign on the kennel door warning that he was vicious. Maybe he had snapped at somebody in the past. Frightened animals with no other recourse or a viable escape route often used their teeth and claws for defense. That didn't make them bad, it merely meant they had been mishandled.

At the end of a row of parked cars, Thor paused, then began to pick up the pace. Hannah kept up by giving him more lead when she fell behind. She could sense the others following her and the thrill of the chase was making her heart pound. Things were about to turn around for them. Thor was going to help apprehend an armed thug and solve Rafe's problems without anybody else being harmed.

Thor strained against his harness. Elated, she started to follow him across the street to an auxiliary parking lot.

An engine roared. Tires squealed. Hannah was jerked backwards in the nick of time to avoid being run over by a speeding SUV.

The leash came out of her grip. She screamed. "Thor!"

Rafe held her tightly by one arm, Lucy by the other.

A sob choked her. She covered her face, afraid to look. Afraid to imagine. "Thor?"

ELEVEN

Because Hannah had buried her face in her hands and Lucy had immediately begun to comfort her, Rafe was the first to see what had actually happened. He was elated. "Look!"

"I can't." Hannah shook her head.

"No. Look." Rafe clasped her shoulders and physically turned her. "See? He's okay."

The big German shepherd cowered barely ten feet away. Rafe crossed the street with the women, still partially supporting Hannah because she seemed unsteady, then released her as she fell to her knees at the curb to embrace her brave dog.

He turned to make eye contact with Lucy. "Did you get a plate number."

"No. Did you?"

Disgusted with himself, he shook his head. "No. I was busy."

"Yes. Thanks. For everything," the older woman said. "If I hadn't seen it I wouldn't believe it. How in the world did that car miss the dog?"

"It had to be by a hair," Rafe said soberly. "If Hannah had been able to hold on he would have been hit for sure."

Teary-eyed, she looked up at him. "I was trying to pull him back." She choked back a sob. "If I had, he'd have been killed." Again, she buried her face in Thor's ruff and hugged him.

To his embarrassment, Rafe found his own eyes growing moist with empathy. Was there a lesson in this? Were his best efforts not being rewarded because there was a better way to proceed? If there was, he sure wasn't seeing it. The would-be assassins escaping in that SUV were undoubtedly on their way to inform Deuce which side of the law he was on, thanks to his casual conversation with Andy. All that effort, all those days spent in prison, all the background created to support his story had been for nothing. Except for a few crooked guards he'd managed to ID while incarcerated, his undercover mission had been a washout.

Bending to take Hannah's arm and urge her to stand he spoke kindly yet firmly. "I hear sirens. We should go."

Lucy agreed. "You two stay here. I'll bring the car."

"No, Gram," Hannah said. "I'm okay and so is Thor. It'll be faster if we go with you."

If Rafe hadn't been in full cop mode he would have told her how proud he was of her bravery and rapid recovery. For a civilian, Hannah Lassiter was behaving with amazing courage under fire, so to speak. Her only flaw, that he'd seen so far, was being too tenderhearted.

Rafe joined Lucy and spoke aside. "She's really something, isn't she?"

The older woman smiled. "You're just now figuring that out?"

"Guess I'm a little slow."

Lucy chuckled. "I'd say so." She took a

few more steps before she asked, "How do you think they located your partner?"

"I don't know, but if we hadn't shown up when we did he'd probably be a goner."

"Yeah. That's what I think. So, there's a leak inside your department, too? I mean, you said there was trouble at the prison. I suppose it's logical to assume others outside are involved."

"I don't like to believe it but you're probably right."

"Thought that's what you'd say." Lucy put out an arm to block him and called to Hannah. "Stop. Now."

"Why?"

"My car," Lucy said, pointing. "The trunk is open. And look at the tires."

Rafe immediately went into a defensive posture and turned with his back to the others. No threats were evident. However, considering the state of their getaway car they were in deep trouble. All four tires had been flattened. There was no way they were going anywhere in that vehicle.

Scowling, Lucy looked at him. "Well, *that's* not good."

"You have a gift for understatement," he said. "Give me your phone and I'll call my superintendent for backup."

"How long will that take?"

"I don't have a clue," Rafe admitted, "but we can't just stand here in the open waiting for the police to shut down the whole hospital."

"True," Hannah said, starting away. "Follow us."

His line of sight took him to her solution and he almost laughed in spite of the seriousness of their plight. The clever dog trainer was on her way to one of the volunteer-run trams the hospital provided to assist patients or visitors who had trouble walking back to their cars.

By the time he and Lucy joined Hannah she had already loaded Thor into the second seat and was waiting for them. An elderly driver wearing a bright yellow vest with the hospital logo was smiling. "Where to, folks?"

While Lucy joined her granddaughter, Rafe sighed and briefly displayed his gun. "Sorry, man. I'm afraid I have to insist that you get out and let me drive."

The man paled and waved his hands in the air as he stepped aside. "Don't shoot. Don't shoot."

"I'll take your vest, too."

"Sure, sure." He shed it quickly.

Rather than reassure him, Rafe chose to simply don the vest over his jacket, slide behind the wheel and press the accelerator. The tram was electric and its top speed was probably ten or fifteen miles an hour. Still, it was better than standing in the midst of the parking lot waiting to be spotted.

"Is this as fast as it goes?" Lucy asked, sounding miffed.

"Yup. Sit back and enjoy the ride."

Hearing Hannah giggle, even a tiny bit, lifted Rafe's spirits. Not much had changed to lessen the danger they faced, yet she had begun to return to her normal self. Once again he was favorably impressed. Someone who had been orphaned and raised by grandparents, regardless of the elders' hidden occupations, should have been less self-assured, less brave, less able to think clearly during stressful periods. Come to think of it, most people would fall apart under constant threat no matter what their backgrounds.

Unfamiliar with the parking lot, Rafe made a turn that took him back toward the door where several patients waited in wheel chairs pushed by more volunteers.

Bypassing them he waved. "Sorry. Full. Catch you next time."

Behind him he heard Hannah laugh again. "You are a chameleon. If I didn't know better I'd have insisted you were the real driver."

"I'll keep that in mind if I ever need to change jobs." Proceeding to a secluded spot at the rear of the sprawling hospital, Rafe stopped the tram and turned to Lucy with his hand out. "Phone."

"Not until I've had a chance to call in a few favors," she said. "Now that Hannah here knows the truth about our family, I figure I may as well take advantage of my connections."

"I thought you were retired," Rafe said.

Lucy paused to pat Hannah's hand and smile before she said, "Some jobs end at retirement, some don't. I like to keep communication open." With that, she stepped spryly out of the tram and walked away, phone pressed to her ear.

When Rafe looked at Hannah's face he glimpsed the concern he'd expected to see before. Yes, she was brave and, yes, she could handle herself well in difficult situations, the same as her beloved grandmother could. Part of that was likely good acting. Hannah was smart enough to realize how desperate their predicament was, yet strong enough to cope with it calmly.

He finally decided to compliment her. "You're doing very well, considering our circumstances."

"Hah!" Shaking her head she grinned at him. "The fun just keeps coming, doesn't it?"

If he hadn't seen the slight trembling of her lower lip he might have been fooled into thinking she was carefree. Of course she was scared. Anyone would be. Even Lucy was probably worried despite her secret agent persona. After all, Hannah was her only close relative and she obviously loved her immensely.

Without pausing to think first, he reached over the back of the driver's seat and touched her hand.

To his surprise she not only didn't pull away, she turned her hand over and laced her fingers through his.

That level of trust and acceptance floored him. Instead of breaking contact he closed his grip and gave her hand a squeeze, unsure whether he was doing it for her or for his own benefit.

Truth to tell, Rafe thought, he'd prefer to enjoy the moment of contact instead of trying to analyze it. Giving comfort had been his intent. Receiving it back in equal proportion was totally unexpected. And nice.

Very nice. Then he looked into her eyes and their shared touch became far more personal.

Hannah didn't want to release Rafe's hand. Ever. Something about the way he was holding her hand was making her feel strangely comforted in spite of their short history. Only the return of her grandmother was enough to make her let go.

Lucy waved her cell phone. "Everybody out of this race car," she quipped. "They'll be looking for it by now and we have real wheels on the way."

Relief flooded Hannah. Keeping her cool and behaving rationally under the present circumstances had taken a lot of effort and she was looking forward to truly relaxing, assuming they would ever be through running.

She'd realized earlier that the only way to survive and prosper again was to eliminate the Fleming gang. As a bonus, when they did that, they would be in position to rescue not only Andy's daughter but hope-

fully many other victims of human trafficking. Recent news reports and even TV
documentaries and movies had made the
public aware of the worldwide problem. It
was going to feel very good to take part
in thwarting the horrible crime. She just
wished she could save every child who had
been taken.

Looking to Lucy, she asked, "Can they
tell you anything about where Kristy might
be?"

When Gram shook her head, Hannah
looked to Rafe. "What about you? Didn't
you say there was some kind of task force
involved?"

"They're how I managed to get sent to
Lyell," he said, shedding the vest and leaving it in the tram. "We know Fleming was
running the operation from prison. Now
that he's out and can do it in person, it's
going to be much harder to break up the
ring."

That reality had been lurking in the recesses of Hannah's mind. Hearing it voiced
caused her actual physical pain. She sighed.

"I am so, so sorry. I tried to reach the new warden ahead of time, but I never managed to get through to him. Somebody always put me off."

"That's interesting to hear," Rafe said. "Did you happen to get a name?"

"No. I assumed it was his secretary. It was a woman."

"I'll pass that on to my superintendent." Once again he reached a hand toward Lucy. "Your phone, please?"

Although she hesitated, she did finally hand it over. "You need—we need—a couple of burner phones. Pay as you go can't be easily traced, if at all, particularly if we destroy them after one or two uses."

"Agreed," Rafe said. "Is this one encrypted?"

"How did you guess?"

In the background, Hannah huffed. "Because you're a spy, silly. You're probably loaded with secret weapons."

"Don't I wish," Lucy said wryly. "I'm afraid I'm all out of exploding pens and cyanide capsules."

"Well, that's a relief."

Leaving the others, Rafe stepped away to make private contact with his superintendent. The call went directly to voice mail. Two subsequent tries had the same result so he gave the phone back to its owner. "No answer. Thanks anyway."

"So, now what?" Hannah asked, looking from one of her companions to the other. "You guys are the pros. Thor and I are just along for the ride." Shaking her head she made a sound of derision. "I must admit it's not nearly as much fun as it looks like on TV or sounds like in books."

"Reality can be unpleasant," Rafe replied. "It can also be awesome when the good guys win."

"Are we?" she asked. "Are we really the good guys when we've had to break the law over and over. I have real trouble rationalizing what we've—what I've—been doing."

"I get it," he said. "I do. The thing is, sometimes it's necessary to step over a line because that's where evil is hiding. Keep thinking about Kristy and all the scared, suffering kids like her and you won't have nearly as much trouble doing whatever is necessary. Fleming and his gang need to be taken down and for some reason we're in a position to do that."

"Are we really?" Hannah was far from convinced. "You've lost your in with Deuce and Gram and I are apparently on a hit list. How is that a good thing?"

"A connection is a connection," Rafe said. "The more they come after us, the greater our chances of catching one or more who will cave under pressure and tell us what we need to know."

"You mean about where Kristy is?"

"Her, and others." He paused. "The more time that passes, the greater the probability she will be flown out of the country. She's a pretty girl and Fleming has bragged that he intends to break up the task force, one way or another."

"Doesn't he realize that the more he hurts people, the greater their desire will be to stop him?"

"He's a sadist. He gets thrills from causing pain in others. At this point I wish I could say he's merely defending his illicit businesses, but I think this has turned into a personal vendetta."

"Against us?"

"Us and the whole task force," Rafe told her. "We have guards on our families and some have even been moved to secret locations."

"What about you?" Hannah asked. "Do you have a family?"

"No," he said, sounding sad.

"Parents? Siblings?"

As he shook his head and made eye contact with her, Hannah realized that he was even more alone in the world than she was. At least she had Gram. Poor Rafe had no one.

"I'm sorry," she said.

"I'm not. Especially in situations like this," he said. "If there is nobody special in my life, they can't hurt me as badly."

"You care about Andy and Kristy, though."

"Yes, I do. I've known her since she was little. That's another reason why we have to rescue her. It's personal for me, too."

TWELVE

If Rafe had had his way, they would have stayed together. Instead, Lucy insisted that she and Hannah separate from him. He might not like the idea but he did see the older woman's logic.

Thor was the giveaway to any observer. Even an untrained eye could tell the big German shepherd was special and his presence painted a bulls-eye on Hannah's back. That was undoubtedly why Lucy had led her off and found them a hidey hole in shrubbery several hundred yards away while he took up a position behind a trash collection array to wait for backup.

He would have been a lot happier if he'd had his own cell phone so he could keep trying the superintendent's private line.

There had to be information of some kind filtering into the station. The more he knew, the better his chances of success—and survival—would be.

A golf cart with two uniformed security guards in it rounded the corner and approached. Rafe ducked back out of sight and peeked between large trash containers.

The driver stopped the cart. He and his partner got out, drew their guns and approached the abandoned tram. They were so intent on repossessing the stolen transport they only briefly scanned their surroundings then ignored them to inspect the tram. He expected them to leave it parked there and call a forensics team but they didn't. One of the guards slid behind the wheel while the other returned to the golf cart and they drove off together.

Luck? No. He didn't believe in luck. He did, however, give credit where it was due so he sent a quick glance into the clouds and smiled. "Thanks."

If he had been running an investigation into the gunshot on the third floor he would have sent someone back to canvas the area surrounding the recovered tram ASAP. With all the police officers now inside the hospital he figured it was only a matter of time before they did just that. Besides, he wanted, needed, to be near Hannah and her grandmother when their replacement car arrived. They weren't going to get rid of him. Not now. Not yet. And certainly not after they had been observed in Andy's room. Fleming already knew who Hannah was and where she and Lucy lived. Deuce was far from stupid. He'd see the connection to law enforcement, put two and two together and find even more incentive to come after them.

Ducking into the shrubbery where he'd last seen the women he expected one of them to answer when he called. "Hannah? Lucy?"

Nothing. Nobody. The old growth was brittle and small pieces had been broken off the hedge. Rafe tried to follow without leaving more signs of passage. Once he was inside the clump of vegetation he could see that it wasn't as dense as it had looked.

He emerged onto a side street, dusted himself off and checked the nearby area. A small strip mall sat across the street while other medical offices filled in the rest of the space. If he was choosing where to go with Hannah and Thor there would be no question.

Checking for oncoming traffic he stepped off the curb.

Rather than call attention to themselves, Hannah had waited outside while Lucy entered the drugstore to buy supplies. There was no hope of replacing everything they'd lost when the car had been robbed, but at least she'd be able to get the extra phones they needed and perhaps energy bars and something to drink. Hannah's mouth was dry and she imagined Thor was thirsty, too.

It seemed kind of silly to be worrying about food when their lives were in danger. Then again, there was nothing like eating a little chocolate to make a person feel better.

Thor had been sitting at her side while she stood behind an array of spring flowers displayed on a tall rack. Suddenly she felt him tense, then stand, bristling.

"What is it, boy? What's wrong?"

The dog took a step in slow motion, as if creeping up on an enemy.

Hannah held him back. Away from Gram and Rafe, with only Thor to defend her, she was very vulnerable.

"This is why wild animals freeze in place when they sense danger," she muttered, letting her own voice soothe her while she watched the K-9 closely for signs of what their next move should be.

Standing hackles on the shepherd's neck and shoulders made him look even larger than he was, and he was plenty big. She glanced between the door to the store and open space on the other side of the flower display. Cars were passing slowly, each one bringing a possible enemy closer. Prior encounters with Fleming's gang led her to believe they would be driving black cars or SUVs. Logic insisted otherwise. Every encounter could be deadly. Every passing car could hold evil personified.

Thor shifted his focus to the left. Hannah's gaze followed. Was that…? It sure looked like Rafe. Nevertheless, she stayed hidden. When Gram was with them she had a lot less trouble relaxing in the company of the supposed convict. His story gibed with Andy's and there were plenty of other reasons to believe him, of course. It wasn't just that. The closest she could describe it was an inner survival instinct. She wanted to trust Rafe completely, really she did.

"Who are you trying to convince?" Hannah whispered to herself. Thor responded by giving her a quick glance before zeroing in on the approaching man and beginning to wag his tail.

Intense relief washed over Hannah like a warm, tropical wave and thanksgiving rippled along her nerves. It was Rafe. And, to her great surprise, she was genuinely happy to see him. So what had become of her caution, her hesitancy? She didn't know and she didn't care.

She heard him call, "Lucy? Hannah?" as she brought Thor to heel and stepped into view.

The instant Rafe spotted her his countenance bloomed into joy, complete with a silly grin. He pivoted then jogged toward her.

There was no way Hannah was going to avoid the kind of fond greeting she expected from him. On the contrary, she was so filled with relief and her own happiness she opened her arms to him and accepted his embrace as if they were long-lost friends.

All he said at first was her name. That was enough, particularly since his tone was so gentle. Their hug was easy, too. Although it didn't last nearly as long as Hannah had hoped, the emotion they shared was clear.

Finally, he set her away, hands on her shoulders. "Hannah. I was afraid I'd lost you."

Blinking back happy tears she tilted her head toward the store entrance. "Gram saw this place and figured they'd have some of the things she wanted so we came over. We were going to go back for you. I know we were."

"I hope so."

"What happened? Did they find the tram?"

"Yes. Some security personnel showed up and took it away."

To her delight Rafe stayed very close, their shoulders almost touching. Hannah agreed with his obvious desire for proximity. She kept Thor on a short lead while she spoke quietly. "I'll be happier once Gram's contacts bring us wheels but I have no idea where we'll go from here, do you?"

Rafe was shaking his head. He slipped one arm around her. "Not a clue. I'm hoping I can get through to my superintendent soon. We're flying blind until we get better intel."

"And word about Andy's daughter," Hannah added. "That has to be everybody's first priority because elapsed time increases the danger to her."

"True." He gave her shoulders a squeeze.

"In one way I'm sorry you're involved, but if you stop and think about it, we do make a pretty good team."

"You and Gram do," Hannah said flatly. She leaned into him, feeling intrinsically connected and drawing strength from him in spite of her earlier misgivings. "I'm not that important."

"Yes, you are. If you and I hadn't gotten involved in the first place, you could have been eliminated as soon as Deuce was free and we wouldn't have federal help, either."

"Surely, the government has its own anti-trafficking forces. Citizens are being transported across state lines and even overseas."

"They do. And we're in contact with them, at least my superiors are. The thing is, you and I and Lucy are boots on the ground, so to speak. Because we're in the thick of things we have different opportunities to break up this particular smuggling ring. It won't end everything. Nothing short of Armageddon can do that. The way I see it, every bite we take out of the system is a victory."

"I can't imagine how scared those young people like Kristy Fellows must be. It's mind-boggling."

"Yes, it is."

Sensing his deepening concern and frustration, Hannah didn't know what to say, how to soothe him. He was right about the unspeakable horrors of the crime they were fighting. It was so vast, so organized, their job seemed insurmountable. Which it was. That wasn't the point, was it?

"So, one Deuce Fleming at a time, right? And then another and another. That's a good thing."

"Humph. Yeah. Let's get the first one behind bars before we celebrate, shall we?"

"Of course."

"Will you be okay if I go inside and look for Lucy? There are a few things I want her to buy for me and she's the one with the money."

Hannah risked a slight smile. "So, what you're saying is that you're going to dump me for a wealthy cougar?"

"Something like that." His mouth twitched as if he was repressing a grin of his own.

"Okay. I'll let you go this time. Just don't forget to come back for me."

"Never," Rafe said soberly, giving her a poignant parting glance. "You're unforgettable in many ways, Hannah Lassiter."

Glad he'd left her without saying more or waiting for her to comment, she watched him walk away. A casual observer wouldn't see anything unusual about him. He was that good at pretending to be carefree and therefore anonymous. She'd called him a chameleon before for good reason. And there lay the conundrum.

Who was he really? Inside all the pretense, what kind of man was Rafe McDowell. For that matter, what was his real name? She doubted it was Rafe. Yes, he was an officer of the law. And, yes, he had been on a covert assignment inside Lyell. That she could accept. The worrisome details now encompassed her personal involvement. As he had said, they needed each other if they hoped to put an end to Fleming's operations, particularly his human trafficking. She was totally on board for that.

When this assignment ended, however, what would become of him? He'd go on to the next job and then the next, wherever he was sent, meaning his presence in and around St. Louis was temporary, at best. Which meant…?

"Do not fall for him," Hannah muttered, knowing she was absolutely right and suspecting it was already too late.

She shook her head and made a face before adding a cynical, "Yeah, right."

Locating Lucy in the store wasn't as easy as Rafe had assumed it would be. Not only was she fairly short, her clothing was nondescript enough for her to blend in with every other regular shopper.

When he finally did spot her he approached quietly. "It would help if you had white hair."

"Take that up with my DNA," she said, frowning at him. "Why are you in here?"

"Hospital security picked up the tram. I figured it was better to join you again instead of waiting to be discovered hiding near the hospital. Why? Were you planning to ditch me?"

"Not at all." Lucy gestured at the shopping cart she was pushing. "I got us some hoodies, new phones and energy bars, flashlights and extra batteries, bottled water and soda pop. What else?"

"Weapons?"

"In a drugstore?"

Rafe nodded. "You could trade those cans for half liters of soda so we'll have the bottles. Go buy matches. And something flammable to use for wicks."

"Not very good for defense," she said.

"Unless we're stuck somewhere. We need gloves, too."

"I have latex ones in the cart."

"Work gloves, too. Hannah's…our hands may need protecting."

"I did think of her needs. They don't have

much of a grocery selection in here. No dog food. I already checked."

"We need to hit a couple of ATMs, too. It's not sensible for you to be the only one carrying cash."

"Already thought of that. The car they're sending us will have new, untraceable credit cards and IDs for all three of us."

"You included me? How?"

That brought a wry chuckle. "You're forgetting who I worked for. Big Brother knows everything about everybody."

"I can't say that's too comforting but in this case it's handy. What else have you done while I was dumpster diving and watching your backs?"

The older woman eyed him up and down. "Not actually diving, I hope. Which reminds me. We need hand sanitizer and wipes."

"And a first aid kit," Rafe added. "A big one."

"The car should be well equipped with things like that," Lucy said. "I'll pick up the rest of the stuff and meet you outside. Go protect Hannah."

"With my life," Rafe said quietly.

Eyes narrowing and jaw clenching, Lucy nodded and said, "I'm counting on it."

THIRTEEN

Seeing Rafe returning without Gram worried Hannah until he explained.

"Okay, fine," she said, resting one hand on Thor's head and wiggling her fingers to scratch behind his ears. "How are we supposed to recognize the good guys or the new car they're bringing? I mean, they're not supposed to look like Secret Service agents in black suits and aviator glasses with listening wires sticking out of their ears, are they?"

Rafe chuckled. "Probably not."

She inched farther behind the rack of spring plants, wishing there was a better hiding place available. "I don't like standing out here like this. One of the St. Louis patrol cars drove through this parking lot a few minutes ago. I didn't realize what the white car was until I saw the blue lettering and picture of the arch on the side."

"Widening the search. I was afraid of that," Rafe said.

"If he comes back he may spot us. You need to go warn Gram and tell her to hurry."

"We could move to a more secure location."

Hannah huffed in frustration. "Oh? Where? I don't see anything except open space." Continuing to monitor the parking lot as she spoke she kept imagining potential enemies. Every vehicle that rolled slowly past sent her pulse racing, even the ones with geriatric drivers, mothers with small children or groups of teens whooping it up.

"School must be out," Hannah remarked, indicating a passing car with the bass of its radio so loud it rattled windows.

Rafe looked at his left wrist out of habit, then shook his head. "I keep forgetting I'm still in prison mode. No watch."

"I've been thinking about that," Hannah said. "What's to keep the police from shooting you as an escaped convict? The news about us and Fleming must be all over the TV and radio." She shivered. "Come to think of it, they're probably hunting me and Thor, too."

"Hopefully, Warden Hotchkiss has taken charge of press releases and we're safe for the present."

"You don't know that he's on our side. And what about the shooting in Andy's room? They probably think we did that, too, in spite of whatever the warden may say. He can't tell them everything without taking a chance on Fleming finding out and tracing us."

"I'm pretty sure that ship has sailed," Rafe said. "From now on we need to look for chances to go on the offensive. Otherwise we'll be running until we make a mistake and he catches up to us."

"That's not very comforting."

"It's not intended to be."

Lucy's return was a relief for Hannah and presumably for Rafe, too. She pushed a loaded shopping cart toward the flower display rack, then ducked behind with the others.

Hannah gave her a hug. "I thought you'd *never* come back."

"I told you I would."

Eager to do something, anything, Hannah grasped her grandmother's arm. "What now?"

"Find someplace away from people where we can safely activate a couple of these phones," Lucy said, gesturing at the plastic shopping bags. "I need to coordinate with my people."

"I thought you already did that," Hannah said, confused. "Aren't we waiting for a car?"

"Such things aren't necessarily easy to provide," she countered, "which is why I bought us all black hoodies. Even in a big city it can take hours to put together a delivery like the one I requested. We don't have spy supply stores on every corner, you know."

As Hannah made a face she was sure she heard Rafe stifling a chuckle. Well, so what? How was she to know how these things worked? Obviously the portrayals on TV and in movies were exaggerated.

"There's no need for the two of you to make fun of me," Hannah said flatly, looking from one to the other. Sadly, neither of her companions argued their innocence, leaving her convinced she was the odd man out. It was as if all the other players in this deadly game knew the rules while she was the one blindfolded and groping in the dark. She might as well have been, she reasoned, given her lack of law enforcement training.

Starting away, pushing the cart, Lucy circled the building. Hannah followed with Thor, assuming that Rafe was behind her. When Lucy halted in the delivery area of the stores Hannah discovered that he was not. Panicky, she searched the distance for him. "Gram?"

Lucy patted the air to wave her quiet. "Hush."

Time seemed to slow to a snail's pace. Finally, Hannah spotted a familiar figure ahead of them. He was gesturing and pointing at a loading dock. Clearly, Gram and the pretend convict had worked out a form of silent communication that she, Hannah, was not privy to. Well, fine. Let them cut her out if they didn't think she was smart enough or capable enough to be included in their subversive actions. As long as they all survived this waking nightmare, she'd swallow her pride and go along with whatever they had in mind. She might not like being excluded, but she'd manage to tolerate it. For now.

Lucy started moving faster, almost jogging behind the rattling shopping cart. Hannah kept pace with Thor trotting obediently at her side. Portions of the pavement were still damp and there were puddles in low spots.

"All right," Lucy said when she was inside the raised concrete sides of the dock. "Good choice." Rummaging in a bag she handed everyone a new hoodie to put on, donned hers, then pulled out two cell phones and gave one to Rafe. "Activate it and call your superintendent."

As Hannah watched, her grandmother opened a second package and began to work with another phone.

"I know how to do that, too," Hannah said. For a few seconds she thought no one had heard her. Then, Rafe reached into the plastic bag and brought out a third phone. Without asking, he passed it to Hannah with a slight smile. "Knock yourself out."

Out of the corner of her eye, Hannah saw Lucy frown at him, but she didn't try to take the phone back. That was a plus. Hannah wanted, needed, to feel useful and valued. Yes, it was a bit selfish. She knew that. It was also a sign that at least one of her companions valued her presence as more than just the human on the end of the leash handling a smart K-9. Properly trained, her dogs filled jobs people couldn't do, of course, such as tracking and intelligent defense. Some had even been used to locate victims buried by disasters or children lost in the wilderness.

The usefulness of the animals wasn't in question. The usefulness of their trainer and handler was. Hannah knew she had an important job to do regarding the dogs' training. What she needed now was to feel just as useful in and of herself.

She smiled at Rafe as she removed the phone's packaging. It was a basic unit which needed a Wi-Fi connection in order to be activated. The others were obviously connecting to nearby sources, probably in the store where Lucy had shopped. Hannah let her device do a search, then chose the strongest signal. Completing the installation and activation slightly ahead of the others gave her ego a tiny boost and brought a grin.

She held up the phone. "Ta-da!"

Gram acted less than impressed while Rafe gave her a thumbs-up and leaned closer to share his screen. "Here's my number. Put it into your phone and give me yours so we can talk if we get separated."

Complying, it occurred to Hannah that separation was a possibility no matter how hard they tried to stay together. The thought of being on her own when assassins were on their trail sent a shiver down her spine. The day had been fraught with danger already and it wasn't over yet. Considering what might take place on the next day and the next was terrifying. It also helped ground her by increasing focus.

"All right," Hannah said when she also had her grandmother's new number. "Somebody please tell me what to expect now. Are we going to stay here or what?"

Pressing the phone to her ear, Lucy turned away to speak more privately. Rafe, on the other hand, put his phone on speaker and let Hannah listen in as he tried once again to contact his superintendent. Her heart hitched when she heard him succeed.

"Yes, Colonel," Rafe said. "Circumstances developed that caused me to join Fleming's escape. It's complicated. I visited Andy and…"

Hannah saw Rafe clenching his jaw and gripping the phone tightly at the muffled sound of an angry tirade. She didn't have to clearly hear each word to know the superintendent was not happy.

"Yes, sir, I am with others at present. No, sir, they're not part of Fleming's gang. I'm afraid that bridge burned when we were overheard at the hospital."

Again, Rafe paused, this time pressing the phone to his ear. Hannah was watching his face and saw his expression changing. Finally, he shook his head and said, "Impossible. With all due respect, Colonel Wellington, I can't."

Hesitating, listening to the cell phone, Rafe said, "Let me rephrase that. I will *not* abandon these people. They are involved through no fault of their own and have helped me as much as I've helped them. We can use this situation to our advantage. I know we can. Fleming is furious at all of us. He's already sent minions to eliminate me and the women. Together, we may survive. Alone, it's less likely."

After a few more moments of listening, Rafe held the phone away and spoke to Hannah. "He wants you and your grandmother to come in so we can protect you."

"What about you?"

"I'll try to complete my mission."

"Without us?" Hannah scowled. Leaning toward his upheld phone, she began a loud protest. "Fleming is mad at me. He's mad at Gram, too. With Rafe we triple the reason he keeps coming back. Taking us out of the picture will cut your chances by two-thirds. That's ridiculous."

Rafe pressed the phone to his ear again, ending her tirade. "She didn't say anything I wasn't thinking. Yes, sir. I know she's a civilian, but the older woman isn't. She's former CIA."

Pulling the phone from his ear as if it hurt, Rafe said, "Whoa! No sir. I'm not joking. She really is."

Hannah looked over at her grandmother and saw that she had been listening to the exchange.

Lucy held up one finger as she continued to speak into her own phone. "Yes. I understand. Unsanctioned. That's fine with me. It's looking like you'll need to contact the head of the Missouri State Troopers and confirm my credentials. Yes, his name is…"

Rafe provided it. "Wellington. Colonel Roger Wellington. His private number is…" He displayed it for Lucy.

"All right," the older woman said. "Tell him to expect a call from DC. It's about time we coordinated this operation, anyway."

"It's about time all right," Hannah said. "I'm not happy being the bait on the end of a line that's being played out with nobody ready to reel it in if the big fish takes the hook."

Next to the drugstore was a nail salon and past that a health food store. The third business was a chain pet shop. When Rafe spotted it his first reaction was relief. He pointed at its rear door. "See if you can get in that way," he told Hannah. "If not, we'll spot for you and tell you when it's safe to walk around front."

"Why?"

"Because you need food for your furry

partner and there wasn't any in the store where Lucy got the other supplies," he said. "It's the perfect cover for you and the dog. If the police start canvassing these businesses you can duck into the dog-washing cubicle and pretend to give him a bath."

"I'm surprised they haven't already done it," Lucy said. "I saw a couple of units cruising the parking lot while I was waiting to rejoin you."

"So did Hannah. It's probably a matter of manpower. The hospital will be their first priority and it will take a while to clear all the floors."

"Okay. We'll go," Hannah said, scowling, "but only because I think it's for the best. If the two of you try to ditch me you'll be sorry."

Lucy gave her a sober look. "Nobody is ditching anybody, is that clear? My handlers know we are working together and so does the state. Parting company now is not in anyone's best interests."

Rafe had led the way to the rear of the pet supply store and was trying the door. "It's locked, as I'd suspected. Besides, Hannah and Thor will look more normal if they use the public entrance." Without waiting for consensus he started off, satisfied when he heard the rattle of the shopping cart on the pitted pavement.

It was closer to retrace their steps from the drugstore so he went that direction. Lack of sirens wasn't necessarily a good sign because all it meant was that the patrol cars had resumed normal activities such as cruising past nearby stores and offices. Even with his superintendent's input he was certain the three of them were still being sought, definitely by Fleming's men and probably by the local police as well. Neither could be allowed to capture them. Not until they were in a position to act to bring down the trafficking ring. How he and his unusual partners were going to do that was beyond Rafe to the extent that he felt the need to rely on divine intervention as well as human aid.

God is in the details, he mused, praying he'd be alert enough, wise enough, to recognize a viable plan when he saw it. One thing was certain. He had been joined to the most unlikely pair of partners imaginable, not counting the addition of a dog, and it was up to him to make sense of their extraordinary team and put it to use.

Peering around the corner he watched passing traffic until enough cars had gone by to assure him the coast was clear. "Now," he called back, gesturing. "Go now."

Hood up, Hannah quickly walked past him then slowed her pace to normal and ambled toward the pet shop.

With Lucy at his side, Rafe continued to scan the traffic. She elbowed him. "Your ten o'clock."

He squinted. "I don't think so."

"Not taking a chance," she said, maneuvering the cart past him and pushing it to the flat red-painted curb that led to the parking lot.

She paused at the edge.

Rafe kept his eye on the dark-colored car that had worried her as it turned down a side aisle and cruised closer. By this time

Hannah had almost reached sanctuary in the pet store.

The driver of the car slowed even more as if looking for a place to park—or for the elusive dog trainer.

In the blink of an eye, Lucy shoved her loaded shopping cart into traffic, let go and screamed.

The vehicle in question came to a halt when its front bumper collided with the cart. Lucy was gesturing wildly and tugging to free the bent cart.

Rafe fully expected the driver to stop and get out to check for damage. Instead, as soon as Lucy pulled the cart back he revved the engine and drove away, not slowing until he had reached the busy street and merged with traffic.

Pausing to watch him go, Lucy turned to Rafe. "She's safely inside?"

He swiveled to check. "Yes. They weren't police so they could have been some of Fleming's men"

"I think it's likely. They didn't recognize

me under this hood so I'm sure they missed seeing Hannah, too."

"They or others like them won't give up."

"I know." The older woman seemed to age right in front of Rafe as her countenance reflected despair. "You'd better go inside with Hannah and get the dog food while I wait for our car. No sense both of us standing out here, especially since you're a wanted man in the eyes of local cops."

Rafe sighed. "You're right. I just hate to leave you, especially after your suicide maneuver with our supplies."

"I have your phone number. I'll lay low and keep you apprised of the situation out here." Lucy managed a wan smile. "Go protect our innocent civilian."

"She won't be so innocent by the time we're done," Rafe said, pocketing the money. "She's learning fast."

Shrugging, Lucy sighed audibly. "Yeah, that's what I'm afraid of. A little knowledge can be worse than none in a life-and-death scenario."

FOURTEEN

"Aww, what a sweet puppy," a patron of the pet supply store said. When the friendly woman reached toward Thor, however, Hannah stopped her.

"Please don't touch him while he's working."

"I'm sorry. I didn't know."

"You can always tell by the vest a dog is wearing. Some will tell you they're in training and others will say what job they're currently doing. See? Service Dog in Training."

"How long does it take?"

Good question. "Right now I'm mostly assessing his skills and temperament. I haven't had him long."

"What do you do if he washes out? I mean, some dogs must not make the grade."

"You're right," Hannah said sadly. She laid a hand atop Thor's broad head. "I have high hopes for this guy, though."

A flash in her peripheral vision caught Hannah's attention and made her jump. Thor picked up on it and backed around her, trembling and staying tight against her legs.

The shopper reacted, too, inching away as if suddenly wary of the power the K-9 possessed. By the time Hannah had soothed him and his hackles had relaxed, they had been joined by Rafe.

"You scared us," Hannah told him.

"I did? Are you sure? He's never acted afraid of me before."

The truth of his words was unsettling. "You're right. I was standing here, talking to a friendly woman, when he acted startled. Funny thing is, I got the same vibes. I suppose I could have been reacting to his fear."

"Or sensed danger without spotting the source," Rafe said.

"Possibly." It was her fondest wish he'd

never have to use the gun Gram had given him, but it was a comfort to note the bump the weapon made resting at the small of his back.

"Let's move to the dry dog food section," Rafe suggested. "We need dinner for Thor and putting one of those big sacks on my shoulder will help hide my face."

Instinctively, Hannah tugged her black hood closer. She would never have thought of disguising herself if Gram hadn't taken charge.

"Know what my problem is?" Hannah asked as they followed Rafe. "I still think like an innocent bystander. You and Gram are more devious."

Rafe gave a soft chuckle. "That's one way of putting it. Personally, I prefer *trained professional*."

Pensive, Hannah trusted him enough to voice her thoughts. "I wonder if I might have chosen a career in law enforcement if Gram had told me the truth when I was younger." Seeing him shaking his head she asked, "What?"

"I don't picture you as a cop."

"Why? Because I'm not smart enough?"

"No, no." As he hesitated, Hannah started to get upset. It was only when he said, "You're too tenderhearted," that she mellowed.

"Who says a person has to be tough to be a good cop? I could train K-9s for the police. Maybe even partner with one. Look at how Thor and I are bonding."

"It's not a question of bonding," Rafe explained. "You've seen dogs that were too stubborn to be taught or too timid." His gaze rested on Thor. "It has more to do with intrinsic strengths and weaknesses."

"And you're saying I'm weak?"

"That's not what I meant, either."

She didn't buy his excuse any more than she believed her grandmother's story about why she'd never revealed the family's background. Neither of her human companions gave her enough credit. In her heart Hannah knew she was courageous and intelligent. She could and would match them in whatever tasks they took on, even the deadly ones. If she had thought for an instant that she was fooling herself she'd have backed off, but she was not about to let herself or her temporary partners—or God—down. Not for a second.

Gram and Rafe had been ordering her around as though she was a clueless child. Well, that was over. She was a member of this strange team and she was going to start acting like it. God would not have included her if He hadn't had a job for her, would He? Of course not. Believers might not always understand divine plans but it was up to them to follow as best they could. She was no different.

Facing Rafe she stood tall, chin up, and demonstrated her decisiveness. "I'm going to wait back here while you buy the food. Get the one in the red and white bag, high-protein, adult mix. Take it out to Gram so we have all our supplies together when our ride gets here."

"I'm sticking to you."

"Then put the food in her cart and come

back in. I don't want to be caught without the proper supplies for Thor."

Although Rafe arched an eyebrow and tilted his head like a curious pup listening to commands he didn't quite understand, he did back away. Hannah saw him approach the brand of dry dog food she wanted and point to it, waiting for her response.

Mouthing *Yes*, she nodded. He slung one of the medium-size sacks over his shoulder and headed for the checkout counter.

Watching him go, Hannah had a brief flash of regret that was quickly replaced by a sense of purpose. She had asserted herself and he had listened instead of arguing. It felt good to be in charge for a change. Very good.

One aisle behind her there were broad windows, a glass-topped door and signs explaining the dog-washing station. Drains in the floor took care of the overflow and soap dispensers stood on a shelf above a raised tub. No one was using the facility at the moment, but there was enough soggy dog hair on the floor to prove it was a popular feature.

She checked her surroundings, saw no other potential bath customers and entered the small room with Thor. He didn't need a bath, but it would be a good time to teach him a few simple commands. Shutting the door behind her kept him in while allowing her to also view the majority of the store.

Nose down, the shepherd investigated the room, checking corners and equipment as if on a mission. Hannah unclipped the leash and let him explore at will to begin with. Then she patted the steps leading to the tub and called his name.

"Thor. Here. Up."

He looked rather confused but interested in what she was doing.

"Up here, Thor. Come on. You can do it." One hand on his collar was enough incentive for him to place his front paws on the bottom step. Hannah didn't rush him.

"That's it. Good boy."

He took one more step then stopped, shivering.

Hannah decided to show him the water spray so she turned it on to hot, waiting for it to warm up, and checked the temperature with her other hand.

Results were almost instantaneous. "Ouch. Hot." She reached toward the cold tap. Thor jumped off the steps and circled her, facing the closed door. His hackles were up and his teeth bared in a snarl. A low growl rose above the sound of the running water.

Hannah whirled.

The man standing in the now open doorway was sneering. "Well, well, what have we here. My old friends."

She was face-to-face with Deuce Fleming!

Thor placed himself at her side, obviously ready to attack. Fleming took little notice. His bulk blocked the doorway. Hannah couldn't tell if there were others with him or if Rafe was on his way back yet. All she knew was that she'd sent her human protector away to bolster her own pride and might be about to pay for her hubris.

Her grip on the shower hose had slackened from surprise, reducing the water to a trickle. *Hot* water. Shouting "No!" she aimed the spray at her antagonist's face and squeezed the handle, sending a scalding stream toward his eyes.

Deuce grabbed his face and doubled over. Hannah slammed into him with her shoulder, managed to pass and saw Thor jumping his prone body in one leap.

She scrambled for the exit. A darkly clad figure made a grab for her as she passed, presenting his wrist as the perfect target for the K-9's canines. One quick nip was all it took to give Hannah a clear path to the front door.

She straight-armed the exit and ran straight into Rafe's arms. He shoved her aside and stood as a human roadblock while she and Thor joined Lucy at the open door of a black SUV that was idling, waiting for them.

Thor didn't have to be told to get in. He beat Hannah and scrambled across the rear seat. Gram gave her a push from behind then slammed the door. "It's Fleming!" Hannah managed to gasp out. "He's in there. We have to get him."

Rafe was way ahead of her. He'd already entered the store, gun drawn. In seconds he was back, panting and scowling. "Lost him. Drive around back."

Lucy accelerated so fast she almost threw Rafe out before he managed to close the passenger door behind him.

Hannah hugged Thor and leaned down to keep them out of the line of fire. Deuce Fleming was mad at her before. Now, bested and shamed in front of some of his men, he was bound to be even more furious. That was good only if it made him careless.

The big SUV slid on a corner, tires screeching. Hannah wanted to know what was happening so badly she chanced a peek. Rafe was braced with one hand on the dashboard, one arm out the open window, ready to fire at Fleming and his fleeing men.

Lucy muttered under her breath.

Hannah pulled herself up more to see why. The alley was empty. And sirens were wailing in the distance.

Rafe pulled his arm inside and lowered the gun. "I can't believe this. We lost them."

One look at Hannah's face told him she was crestfallen. Her words affirmed it. "It's my fault."

"Pinning blame is useless," Lucy said. "Now that we know he's still in the city, we can inform law enforcement. Who knows. Maybe they'll spot him for us."

"It would help if we knew what they're driving," Rafe said. "It must be fast."

"Don't let this car fool you," Lucy said. "There's plenty under the hood if we need it, just no sense racing around and calling attention to ourselves if we don't have good reason."

In the back seat Hannah sniffled. Rafe sent her a smile. "Don't worry about it. We'll get him. What happened in there, anyway?"

When she related the story of the hot

water, he chuckled. "Serves Deuce right. He should know better than to underestimate you. I wish I could have seen you scald him."

"I wish the water had been a lot hotter," she said honestly before recanting. "Sorry. I shouldn't have said that."

"Why not?"

"Because it's mean. I don't want to sound vindictive."

"See what I was trying to tell you?" Rafe said with a hint of tenderness. "You don't have the right temperament to be a cop."

"I defended myself when it counted."

"Yes, but then you wished you hadn't."

"Uh-uh. I never meant that exactly. I wasn't sorry I acted, I was just sorry I enjoyed it so much."

That brought laughter from Lucy. "Might be best if you didn't try to analyze yourself too much until this is over," she said, grinning. "We do what we do for many reasons, some of them not the best. Never beat yourself up for survival instincts. Those come with humanity. You wouldn't be normal if you didn't choose sides in this war."

"War?" Hannah asked.

Rafe agreed. "Yes. A war against evil. It's been going on forever. We have to keep trying, keep fighting, even if the enemy seems to be winning. Every battle counts. That's what I meant before."

"I get it," Hannah said. "I do. I just feel so outnumbered."

"Which we are," Lucy said, sobering. "I'm going to put some distance between us and this last episode so we don't get pulled over and arrested because of the altercation and brandishing a gun. I want to finish what we started and I think my friends in high places may be able to help."

"By tapping into the closed-circuit cameras at the strip mall?" Rafe asked, expecting to be correct.

"Hah! That's kid stuff." As she steered into passing traffic, Lucy floored him by saying, "Satellite observation. I can give my people the proper coordinates, tell them what times to look, and have a clear enough picture of Fleming's getaway car to read the letters on the license plate."

"Whoa. Are you kidding?"

She laughed, made eye contact with her granddaughter in the back seat and winked. "I would never joke about something like that. The idea of an eye in the sky may not be comforting to regular people but it's invaluable to folks like us."

"Once they ID him, do you think they'll be able to find him in this sea of cars?" Hannah asked.

Rafe answered. "In this case, that is my fondest hope."

"It was mine, too, until I was face-to-face with him," Hannah admitted. "Right now I'd rather the police picked him up and I never had to see him again."

"As long as they can get him to reveal where he sent Kristy," Rafe reminded her. "Time is running out for her."

FIFTEEN

Once out of downtown and on the highway, Hannah got her bearings from the famous Gateway Arch that rose 630 feet above the banks of the Mississippi River. Night had fallen and with it came much cooler temperatures.

She shivered and hugged Thor to share warmth. It helped that he had chosen to drape himself across her lap and had finally relaxed enough to doze. Truth to tell, her own eyelids felt so heavy she had to fight sleep.

"I'm going to pull into a parking garage so we can all get some rest," Lucy said.

Hannah met her gaze in the rearview mirror. "Sorry. I can't seem to keep my eyes open."

"You expended a ton of energy today," Rafe said. "We all did. Resting, even for a few hours, will help us stay at the top of our game. We can't afford to let ourselves function at less than our best."

"It feels like it's been weeks since the prison break," Hannah said, yawning.

Lucy huffed. "You've got that right. We've been through enough to wear out a marathon runner." She took the next off-ramp. "First we'll pick up some hot food and then I'll find us a place to lay low."

"I'll need to feed and walk Thor, too," Hannah said. The mention of his name caused the big shepherd to lift his head and look at her. She quieted him with a gentle pat and he closed his eyes again.

"I need to advise my boss, too," Rafe said, "and find out if Andy's okay. That hospital fiasco has to have taken a lot out of him."

"It's nothing that finding his kidnapped daughter won't fix," Lucy offered. She looked at Hannah again. "How are you doing? Truly, not what you think we want to hear."

"I'm tired, of course." She managed a genuine smile as she pondered her state of mind. "It's kind of scary how being afraid and then winning a battle against the bad guys is starting to appeal to me. That's counter intuitive, right? I mean, why should I be thinking about facing Deuce Fleming again when I already said that was the last thing I wanted?"

"Because you're beginning to believe we can beat him," Rafe said. "That bothers me."

"Why?"

"Promise you won't get mad again?"

"Promise," Hannah told him.

"Okay. It's unsettling because it means you may act too brave when your previous escapes weren't due to skill. Face it, Hannah, you were fortunate to survive. More than once. Please don't count on yourself to bring him down. It's going to take a team effort and outside aid to end his reign of terror for good. We thought we'd done that before and he managed to run his operation from inside Lyell."

"I understand what you're saying. Really I do. It's just, I don't know...exciting?"

Lucy tut-tutted and looked over at Rafe. "We should have figured out a way to leave her behind."

"Well, it's too late now," he replied. "Fleming has to be out of his mind about the scalding she gave him. There's no way he'll give up until he's in custody."

"And maybe not then," Hannah added. "I know. Just remember who made the first mistake that started all this."

No one rebutted that statement, nor had she expected them to. Fleming had so successfully coerced her that she'd gone against her sense of right and wrong and broken the law. That was how she and Gram had gotten sucked into this mess. Only Rafe was involved on purpose and that for a good cause, meaning none of the blame rested on him.

Conversation ebbed until they had ordered and picked up their food to go. The enticing aromas roused Thor. He and Hannah ducked instinctively when the SUV entered a dimly lit parking structure. The spot Lucy chose for their respite was at the very top in a far corner. Hannah didn't realize she'd been barely breathing until they stopped.

Thor was antsy so she leashed him and immediately got out of the car, prepared to clean up after him, while the others divvied up the meals. It was good to be away from the reality of the vehicle, even for a few short minutes. Part of her wanted to be an active participant in the manhunt and rescue of Kristy, while another part of her wished she could just walk off into the night and be done with everything. She couldn't, of course. It didn't take an expert theologian to imagine the reasons why. And it didn't take a cop or a former spy to convince her of the danger. She knew. She'd always known, deep down inside.

Looking back, Hannah could see how her choice to minister to convicts via the dog rehab program had set the stage for this current drama. The initial error lay in who had gotten permission to participate, not in the idea, itself. Other prisons supported similar outside aid with great success. Hers had been wonderful for the first couple of years.

Suddenly truth hit her. Rafe had been right. She was as much a victim of Deuce Fleming and his cohorts as poor Andy was. Their lives had been affected beyond reason when Fleming had become involved. He was the catalyst. They had to take him out, one way or another, or his list of victims would grow.

Hannah closed her eyes and prayed. "Father, thank You for putting the three of us together this way. Please help us, help me to be who You want me to be and do what You put me here to do. Stay with us, Jesus. We trust in You." And she did. With all her strength.

She looked back at the parked black SUV and her heart swelled with emotion. With thanksgiving. The two people she was with were perfect for the job they all faced.

Therefore, she could count herself as capable, too. They would do this, whatever it cost. Go wherever the tasks took them. Win.

Fortified, changed and reassured, a new Hannah stood tall and started back toward the car.

Rafe had rolled down his window to listen and watch over Hannah and Thor from his vantage point in the front seat. If she had strayed too far away he would have gone after her, of course. That went without saying. The only reason he hadn't insisted in the first place was because he'd sensed her need to be alone and think.

In the interim, Lucy had received a report from her insiders. Fleming had chartered a private plane and made plans to leave the country, ostensibly with a group of young women who had volunteered for charity work abroad. Consensus was that many of these women had been either kidnapped or coerced. Everyone's hope was that Kristy was among them and therefore still in the States.

He handed Hannah a fresh alcohol wipe to clean her hands before passing her the paper sack containing her burger and fries. "Water or soda?" he asked her.

"Water, please. And one of those empty plastic boxes so I can let Thor drink, too." She put it on the floor for him, smiling when he splashed her foot. "My back seat buddy is a messy drinker."

"Just make sure you don't accidentally lose your burger to him," Rafe warned lightly. "He's looking at it like a hungry wolf."

"Distant ancestor," she quipped. "I'll be careful. Dogs can't have onions. They're really bad for them."

"I didn't know that." Facing forward he took pains to remove any trace from a bite of his own meal before holding it out for the K-9. "Is this okay?"

Hannah nodded. "Yes. Okay, Thor. It's okay."

The dog's whole mouth closed over the

ends of Rafe's fingers with an audible snap. "Whoa! Easy boy. I need that hand."

"Next time you want to feed him, give it to me and I'll work on his manners."

"Good idea," Rafe said as he cleaned his hand with another of the sanitary wipes. "He's all yours."

Laughing, she ate more before breaking off a piece of bun. This, she offered in a closed fist so Thor had to be gentle to nose it out. By the third bite he looked as if he'd learned.

Rafe waited until she'd finished eating before he began to fill her in on the latest details. "Our friends with the spy in the sky located the vehicle that got away from us and traced it to an old hotel outside town."

"Really? Are we going there?"

"Not right away," Lucy said. "We need to give our people time to get into position before anybody approaches."

"We can't wait, Gram. What about Fleming? What if he escapes or hurts Kristy?"

"We're counting on the fact that she's too valuable an asset to lose," Lucy said with conviction. "He's planning to fly abroad the day after tomorrow. According to reliable intel he's waiting for the arrival of another batch of victims so they can all go together."

"He must be awfully sure of himself."

Rafe agreed. "He is. Always has been. My people are watching the airfield. He won't get by them even if he changes plans and tries to leave early."

"What if he drives?"

"We have that covered, too," Lucy said. "What we need to do now is to get some sleep so we're ready for tomorrow."

Frowning, Rafe caught her attention and gave a slight shake of his head to keep her from explaining further. There was more to the infiltration strategy the two agencies had been discussing and if they stuck with the notions they'd already presented, rest for Lucy and for him was imperative. So was keeping the details from Hannah until just before executing the risky plan. He had no doubt she was going to object in the strongest of terms and he wanted to save arguments for last.

Sighing, he leaned his head back against the seat and pictured Hannah the moment she learned that a female law enforcement officer was going to take her place in the assault on the hotel. She was bound to go ballistic and he was not looking forward to trying to talk her down.

Sleep eluded Hannah—for about five minutes after she finished eating. Warm food and the plush seats soothed and calmed her.

Thor curled up beside her and she rested one hand on his shoulders knowing that any disturbance would rouse him instantly. Reassured by that knowledge she sank into a deep sleep beyond dreams and awoke to see the sun rising outside the parking structure.

Yawning, she stretched and looked around. Lucy and Rafe stood at a concrete railing. Because they were facing the eastern sky they were surrounded by haloes of warm light as if caressed by the morning. Their body language, however, did not carry the same image of peace. Lucy was leaning toward him, acting intent on making a point. He was shaking his head.

Hannah snapped the leash on Thor and climbed out. The change in her companions when they saw her was unquestionable. They not only stepped apart, both were acting nonchalant, *acting* being the key word. She smiled. "Good morning. What's up?"

"We were just waiting for you," Rafe said.

Lucy agreed. "Right. There's a public restroom on the ground floor." She pointed. "Elevator's over there. Want me to hold the dog for you?"

"No. Thanks. Thor needs to be walked anyway. We'll be back in a jiffy."

"I'll go with you," Rafe said. "Lucy can drive down and pick us up at street level. Then we can go grab breakfast."

His forced casual attitude gave Hannah the shivers. "Has there been any word on Fleming?"

"Not since last night," Rafe said.

She didn't quite believe him so she raised

an eyebrow. "Really? Neither one of you even asked?"

"I did check in," Lucy offered. "There wasn't much to report. No activity at the airfield."

"What about that hotel they were watching?"

Rafe took her elbow and urged her toward the elevator. "I'll fill you in while we ride down."

With a parting glance at her grandmother, Hannah complied. It was clear something was up although neither of her companions seemed as nervous as she figured they'd be if danger was imminent. Instead, they were acting reluctant to engage with her, as if there was some secret between them that was being kept from her, in particular.

She stepped onto the elevator with Thor, pleased that his hesitation at the threshold was brief. The door slid closed. She turned to Rafe. "Okay. Let's have it. What's going on?"

"I don't know what you're talking about."

"I don't believe you. And I don't believe

Gram, either. You two are up to something behind my back. Now what is it?"

Unfortunately, the elevator reached the ground floor and the doors opened before she got an answer so she stopped him as soon as they'd stepped clear. "Well?"

"It's not carved in stone. It's just…" He made a face. "Listen, it's not something we sanctioned, okay? The feds and state people are basically running this op now."

"And?"

Shrugging, Rafe stuffed his hands into the pockets of his jacket. "And, they've decided to use only trained personnel for the infiltration."

"So?" She didn't like the feeling she was getting or the ideas flying through her head. Were they cutting her out? After everything she'd done and the way she'd stood up to Fleming on her own, were they actually going to force her to step away?

"So, we'll be met at the Randolph Bend of the Missouri River by members of the primary assault team. One of them will be a policewoman who resembles you as closely as possible. She'll take over with Thor and stand in for you if it turns out we're needed. They figure, with the dog involved, Fleming's men won't question the handler's identity."

"This substitute is a K-9 officer?"

"Um, I don't know. I guess so. I mean, I've never met her."

"That's what I figured." Facing Rafe she spoke her mind. "People tend to underestimate somebody like me. Because I make the job look easy they think anybody can step into my shoes and do things just as well as I do. Well, they can't. You and Gram should know that. You've seen proof."

"It wasn't our idea."

"Doesn't matter. Did you protest? Did you try to explain that I have certain skills worth considering? "

"We weren't invited to discuss it," Rafe countered. "We were just told about the plan and thankful to be allowed to be present." He paused, apparently choosing his words carefully. "They could have cut us out completely."

"You mean like they're cutting *me* out?"

Hannah could tell it cost him dearly to say, "Yes."

SIXTEEN

Tension inside the unmarked SUV was so high Rafe was surprised the air wasn't actually vibrating. His senses were heightened by what they were about to do and he could tell that Lucy felt the same. As for Hannah, well, she was harder to read. Not that she was a good actress, he concluded. It was more a case of her emotions being on a roller coaster ride. At the topmost portion of the tracks she could be elated. Anybody could. It was when the coaster carried her to the bottom of the loops and turns that she seemed withdrawn and he hadn't decided whether that meant anger or depression.

In many ways, Rafe would have preferred that Hannah showed she was mad at their group's plans even if that meant she was also furious with him and Lucy. Anger tended to heighten a person's awareness while being down in the dumps had the opposite effect.

Outlying portions of St. Louis had swallowed up a small historic settlement on Gabaret Island, one mile south of the confluence of the Missouri and Mississippi Rivers, yet it had somehow managed to retain its name and a spot on the map. Explorers Lewis and Clark would undoubtedly be shocked at the way their campsite had changed after more than two hundred years.

"My GPS indicates we can drive across if we go north and use the bridge to Chouteau," Lucy said.

"Where is our first rendezvous taking place?" Rafe asked her.

"Off Highway 70, a little way from the arch, where we won't be so likely to draw attention," the older woman answered. "Once we're on the island there's only thirteen hundred acres to hide in."

"Where are you supposed to be dumping me?" Hannah asked, sounding beyond miffed.

Lucy frowned at Rafe. "You should never have told her."

"It was only fair," he countered. "She's been with us from the beginning. She *was* the beginning."

"Yes, well, I can't say I'm unhappy about taking on a substitute human target for the Fleming gang to shoot at," Lucy said. Hannah met and held her gaze in the rearview mirror but didn't comment.

Rafe could tell she was upset without becoming irrational. That was a definite plus. Convincing her to step away at this last crucial juncture might not be as hard as he'd anticipated. One of the reasons he'd told her details of the plan ahead of time was to give her a chance to think things through and accept the inevitable. Fortunately, it was beginning to look as if that was exactly what she'd done.

Swiveling in his seat as far as possible without removing his seatbelt, Rafe looked back at Hannah. Her features were as pretty as ever but there was a disquieting glint in her eyes. "I really am sorry about this. You know I'd have included you if it was possible. After all you've been through you deserve to be in on the capture."

"I'm glad somebody realizes that." He saw her gaze dart to the back of her grandmother's head for an instant. "I'm not the orphaned Lassiter kid anymore. I don't need coddling."

"Loving and protecting you is *not* coddling," Lucy shot back. "You will always be my precious grandbaby."

"I'm not a baby," Hannah said. "Not anymore."

Rafe decided it was time to interrupt. "Okay, ladies, let's talk about where we're going and what's expected of us when we get there."

Hannah huffed. "Why tell me?"

He ignored the gibe. "Members of law enforcement attempted to infiltrate the hotel staff and failed. None of Fleming's people could be bribed or coerced so they don't have anyone inside who can pass them the

information they need for the final takedown."

"Why not just storm the place?" Hannah
asked. "They know where Deuce is and
where the victims are, don't they?"

"That's part of the problem." Rafe looked
to Lucy, wanting her okay to proceed.
When she merely gripped the steering
wheel and stared at the road ahead he continued anyway.

"We believe that the people we want to
rescue, including Kristy, are being held
somewhere else. They're supposed to be
brought to the hotel and then leave with the
Fleming gang."

"You're sure?" Hannah asked.

Shrugging, Rafe said, "As sure as we
can be. Listening devices on the outside
have picked up most of what we know. It
looks like Fleming's pride is going to be his
downfall. He wants to be able to personally march those prisoners aboard the plane
so they'll all know who's the boss. If he'd
shipped them off in smaller bunches we
might have already missed saving some."

"I don't get why he chose to rendezvous on Gabaret. I'd think he'd be safer in a much more crowded area the way you're planning on meeting the strike team."

"Overconfidence, I think," Rafe said. "After everything he's gotten away with, in and out of prison, I suspect he's feeling invincible."

"I suppose it's possible. He never struck me as foolish, though. I mean, look how he manipulated me."

"That success undoubtedly bolstered his ego which is another element in our favor."

"And a very good reason why the takedown should include me," Hannah argued.

Studying her expression as he commiserated, Rafe was certain she had come to terms with the inevitable change about to take place. One side of him wanted to continue to work beside Hannah. A more practical side insisted it was wiser to leave her behind and substitute an armed, trained professional. Assuming his goal was to protect Hannah, and it was, he had to choose leaving her behind. The problem was how to justify that conclusion without reveal-ing how fond of her he'd grown in the short time they'd spent together. It was bad enough that he, himself, knew.

If they hadn't been currently confined to the car he'd have taken her hand again and led her aside to privately explain his di-lemma. He could do that later. He *would* do it. In the meantime he stared through the windshield and wondered how such a clear, beautiful morning could be so fraught with danger, with the very real threat of death.

"Not Hannah," Rafe prayed in a whisper that was muted by the roar of the power-ful engine. He blinked to clear his vision. "Please Lord, watch over Hannah."

That prayer was still echoing in his mind when Lucy pulled off the highway and into a spacious, busy truck stop.

Rafe kept checking and assessing their surroundings until he spotted a handful of white patrol cars and a mobile command center van with a satellite dish mounted on its roof.

If he had been positive there were no

double-minded officers in this group he might have actually been able to let down his guard enough to relax.

Watching her grandmother and Rafe greeting the officers at the command center vehicle, Hannah took a deep breath and sighed once before leashing Thor. "Okay big boy, you behave now, you hear?"

Panting, he seemed to smile up at her.

"That's a good boy. Let's go."

In no hurry to relinquish control of the basically untrained K-9, she stepped out of the SUV. Thor was behaving as though he had accepted her authority. What he might do if they were physically separated was another story. Besides, she reasoned, Deuce Fleming knew what she looked like. He'd been in her training classes at Lyell. How any substitute expected to fool him was beyond her.

Nevertheless, she did respect the police and the tough job they were tasked with doing. Under her breath she murmured a surrender prayer and approached the people Gram and Rafe were speaking with.

A man wearing a black protective vest over totally nondescript black clothing nodded to acknowledge her and went on addressing the others. "We're waiting for news from our spotters on the arrival of the victims. They're being delivered in small batches, which is why we didn't move in sooner. Once Fleming knows we're on to him and his operation he'll stop everything and we might lose any who haven't already arrived."

"You don't have info on all branches of his organization?"

"We know a lot. Trouble is, we can't be sure we're not missing anybody."

That made sense to Hannah. Sort of. If she had been in charge she knew she'd have wanted to storm the hotel ASAP and clearly that was not for the best. *Which is why they're running things and I'm not,* she told herself. In the background she noticed a young woman whose build and hair color were similar to hers. Although this woman wore the same kind of protective vest the other team members did, she wasn't in uniform.

Hannah tightened her hold on Thor's leash. Sensing her nervousness the dog pressed his shoulder to the side of her leg and leaned in. She rested her free hand atop his broad head to comfort him and spoke softly. "It's okay, boy. It's okay."

But it wasn't, was it? The dog might not know they were about to be separated, but he'd sensed tension in the atmosphere around the group of vehicles.

The agent in charge motioned to her. "Bring the dog."

"Thor, heel," was all Hannah said, starting forward. She was met halfway by the woman officer she'd noticed.

"My name is Layla," the policewoman said, taking off aviator sunglasses, then offering her hand.

Hannah shook it reluctantly. "This is Thor. Please understand. He's new and hasn't had a lot of training. He understands basic commands, just don't make the mistake of counting on him the way you would a fully vetted working K-9."

Scowling, Layla turned to her superior. "I thought you said the dog was a pro."

"We thought he was." Stepping aside he spoke into his radio, then returned. "We'll use him anyway."

Layla held out her open hand. It was all Hannah could do to force herself to pass the leash. Once the officer had assumed command she gave a tug. "C'mon, dog."

Thor sat on his haunches and refused to leave Hannah's side.

"Tell him to come with me," Layla ordered.

"Even if I do that and he obeys here and now, what's to say he'll act normal later when you need him? Deuce not only knows my face, he's seen me handling Thor. No matter how good your disguise is, you can't fool the dog and that means you won't fool Fleming and his men, either."

When Layla wrapped a length of Thor's leash around her hand and dragged his paws across the asphalt, Hannah had had enough. "Stop that. You'll hurt him."

"Then do something about him," the female officer said in a raised voice that was attracting the attention of her fellow officers as well as passersby.

"Give me that." Hannah jerked the leash from her hand and resumed command of the frightened shepherd. Together they approached and faced the agent in charge. "The dog stays with me."

"We want to use him as part of this operation. If I'd known he wasn't properly trained I'd have had another German shepherd standing by."

"Well, you don't. You have Thor and you have me. I've worked one-on-one with Deuce Fleming, and even with those sunglasses on, your substitute won't pass for me. We both know it. Otherwise, why would you insist on using Thor to convince him?"

Up to now, she had been ignoring Rafe and Gram. Now, she looked to both of them.

"Tell him. Make him understand how right I am for this job."

Seeing them look at each other for long, silent moments Hannah was afraid they wouldn't back her up. Then, in unison, they said, "She's right."

Hannah was far too nervous to continue pleading her case so she simply stood there under the scrutiny of the top agent and tried to appear unruffled.

Finally, he motioned to Layla. "Give her your vest and earbud."

"But, sir…"

"We have to take a chance." He pointed to Rafe and Lucy. "These two are experienced enough for all three of them. We're closer to breaking up this trafficking ring than we've ever been and I'm not about to let a four-legged problem mess things up. Lassiter goes with the dog."

Hannah's heart cheered and she grinned so broadly her cheeks hurt. They were going to let her help avenge her murdered parents and make up for all the sacrifices Gram had made raising her. Moreover, she was going to get the chance to help Rafe rescue his partner's daughter. Having met Andy, she knew how desperately Rafe needed to accomplish that, to be directly involved in not only solving the kidnapping but to also make amends for Andy's on-the-job injury while they were working together.

A sudden shiver snaked up her spine and prickled the hair at the nape of her neck. She had just talked her way back into imminent danger and it was dawning on her that she was about to walk smack into the presence of the man who hated her most in all the world. Plus, there was Thor to think of.

"*That's* why I need to go," she muttered to herself, following Gram and Rafe back to their SUV. "The others are here to rescue people. I'm here to look after this loyal dog."

That conclusion made perfect sense. It also made her tremble all the way to her core and left her mouth so dry she could barely swallow.

What she didn't expect when she climbed into the vehicle with Thor was a barrage of intense chastisement from the very people she was there to help.

SEVENTEEN

Lucy led the tirade so well Rafe didn't feel the need to do anything but agree. "What did you think you were doing back there, huh? Don't you realize that taking care of you will put the rest of us in jeopardy?"

"I've done all right so far," Hannah reminded her grandmother.

"Hah! You may be a crack shot but paper targets are a lot different than human ones."

"I could give her a crash course in tactics while you drive," Rafe offered.

"And accidentally shoot me through the seat back? No thank you."

The more he thought about it, the better he liked his idea. "No bullets. I'll make sure the gun is empty. I just want to see how she handles it in case of emergency."

"Gram was right, I could never shoot anybody," Hannah said.

"You could hold someone at bay who didn't know you were so softhearted."

It surprised him when she joked, "At least you didn't say softheaded or wimpy."

"There is nothing wimpy about you," Rafe assured her with a slight smile. "If anything, you're too brave. Put that vest on under your hoodie so they can't tell you're protected."

Pausing as she complied, Rafe did the same with his. Lucy had already hidden her protective clothing like the old pro she was.

"Okay," Hannah said, smoothing the soft black fabric over the top of the bulky vest. "I just have one question."

"Shoot."

She snorted a chuckle. "Lousy choice of words. What I want to know is what happens if they don't shoot me in the middle of my body where this thing protects me? Huh? What then?"

Rafe answered, "You get hurt. Badly. So I suggest you plan to duck as often as possible. Best-case scenario, if we get captured, would be getting thrown into the holding cell with the prisoners so we could tell them they were about to be rescued and try to confirm that they're all there."

"Terrific. What makes you think they'd let us keep our cell phones to report to the strike team?"

He produced a tiny black object and held it out to her. "They won't. That's what this is for. It clips onto fabric and transmits up to a mile under ideal circumstances." He fitted a pliable receiver into his ear and handed one to Lucy. "These will pick up what's being said without any action on your part."

"Any crook worth his pay will find it on me."

"I agree," Rafe said soberly. "That's why you're going to pin it on the inside of Thor's harness. Only a fool would try to frisk a dog."

Seeing the sparkle in her eyes and the lopsided smile she was obviously trying to subdue endeared her to him. This was no normal woman. Hannah was so special he had no words to adequately describe her. She had adapted so well to their situation, it was akin to working with a fellow officer. Tenderhearted or not, she had what it took to do this job and do it well. She was intelligent, brave and quick-witted.

And adorable, his mind added. No argument there.

Tempted to voice his thoughts he spoke to Lucy, instead. "Pull over for a sec so I can trade seats with Thor and teach Hannah how to safely handle an automatic."

"The Glock I gave you?"

"Yes."

She produced a smaller pistol and also handed that to him. "Use this one. It's easier to work the slide. I had to switch to a smaller caliber when arthritis weakened my grip."

He accepted the extra gun, got out and waited until Hannah had sent Thor over the center console into the front passenger seat before he joined her. Judging by the way she was frowning, she was not thrilled with the lesson he was about to give while Lucy continued driving toward Gabaret.

Rafe emptied both guns and checked to make sure there was no ammo left in the chambers after he dropped the clips. "First rule, never point a gun at anything unless you plan to shoot it."

"Well, duh. I know that. So, how am I supposed to hold anybody at bay if I don't aim at them?" Hannah made such a ridiculous face he almost laughed. Instead, he said, "Okay. One exception. Just keep your finger off the trigger and lay it beside the trigger guard like this. See? It never touches the trigger unless you're ready to fire."

As he handed it to her, empty, he felt her tremble as his fingers brushed against hers. Truth to tell, he wasn't feeling all that steady about it either. To help distract himself, he concentrated on watching her hands and continuing the lesson. "Here's the safety on this gun. It's almost the same as the other weapon. You can disengage it with your thumb."

It pleased him that Hannah was able to

follow his orders and had the grip strength to pull back the slide and chamber a round in the larger Glock 9mm. With his encouragement she handled both guns appropriately—until he reloaded them. Then, she acted as if she was holding a live rattlesnake. "I thought you were used to firearms."

"I am," she countered. "It's just different when I think about harming somebody."

Rafe reclaimed the guns, checked the clips before replacing them, then passed Lucy's to her over the back of the seat. "Lesson finished. Too bad this isn't the time or place to do some live firing so I can check her accuracy."

Snorting, the older woman tucked the gun into her belt. "Trust me. She's got good aim. The question is whether or not she's got the guts."

"Don't be so cynical," he warned, hoping the disparaging remark didn't undermine Hannah's confidence. He had no way of knowing what they were about to face or whether she'd need to actually use the gun to defend herself, but he hoped she'd never be tested under fire.

"I won't chicken out," Hannah chimed in. "I promise. But shooting at somebody is going to be a last resort." The wisp of a smile she gave Rafe grew broader when she added, "I'd much prefer swinging a frying pan or a baseball bat if I have to fight back."

"Let's hope and pray this assignment is nothing like that," Rafe said, almost ready to smile in spite of the circumstances.

When Hannah added, "Or steaming hot water from a doggie spa," he broke into a grin. "You are really something, you know that?"

From the driver's seat he heard Lucy muttering. "We all need our heads examined."

Sobered, Rafe stowed his Glock, reached for Hannah's hands and clasped them in both of his. "What we're about to do is very dangerous. You do realize that, don't you?"

"Meaning we could die? I get that. I also don't think it's my time to go."

"Nobody ever does." Her grip on his fingers tightened as if she meant to comfort so he held fast, too. Unshed tears glistened in her eyes, making his own begin to water in spite of the macho image he carefully maintained. This woman got under his skin the way no one else ever had and he sensed a shared empathy that unnerved him. She understood how important it was to him to rescue Kristy and how Lucy had waited half a lifetime for the chance to avenge Hannah's parents, but that wasn't all. Somehow, Hannah had tapped into his heart and made herself at home there.

Rafe was loathe to accept his feelings for her, yet there they were. Undeniable. Unfathomable. And, God help him, unacceptable. Once this current danger was past and their reasons for being together ended, he'd go his way and Hannah would go hers. Parting was inevitable. So was a cooling of the emotional attachment they had formed due to this assignment. He'd seen it happen before. He'd even taken part in psychological debriefings to help him come down from the highs created by danger. To put it into layman's terms, cops and firefighters could get addicted to adrenaline the same way skydivers and race car drivers did.

And when it was over, it was over, he reminded himself. Thinking about the future in the midst of what could be a deadly assignment was a futile exercise. Truthfully, they had only this moment in time and no more.

Without taking time to rationalize his actions, Rafe lifted their joined hands between them and kissed the backs of Hannah's fingers.

She touched his forehead with her own and they sat that way, head to head, for longer than Rafe had intended. It was a beautiful moment, one he would have maintained longer if Hannah had not leaned her head on his shoulder and sighed.

He was lost. Overwhelmed. Releasing her hands he slipped one arm around her shoulders and pulled her into a tender embrace regardless of the sounds of derision coming from the retired government agent behind the wheel.

* * *

Hannah's heart was racing, her breathing ragged—and all she was doing was sitting there beside Rafe. If she was already this agitated, how in the world was she going to cope when the operation actually got underway?

Traffic was at a standstill approaching the bridge north of their destination. Everything seemed normal until she saw Lucy slam a fist into the steering wheel. Worse, Gram seemed to be unduly concerned about something behind them.

Rafe leaned forward. "What is it? What do you see?"

"Not sure." Her glance kept shifting between vehicles behind her and the reason for the blocked roadway ahead. "I'd like to know if this tie-up is thanks to our people or for some other reason. I don't like being trapped."

"Looks like actual construction to me," Rafe said. "The state has been doing a lot of infrastructure repair lately."

When Hannah saw Lucy tilt her head as

if questioning, she shivered. If Gram was worried then she was worried, too. Still, anything that delayed their progress should also hamper Fleming's plans so it couldn't be all bad. Or could it?

The line of cars was moving slowly. Men with signs and walkie-talkies took turns letting a few vehicles through. Hannah studied the faces of the workers, looking for anything off-putting or familiar. Nothing seemed amiss.

"They look legit to me," she murmured, surprised when Rafe said he agreed.

"I'll call it in just the same," he added. "Can't be too careful."

Watching and listening, Hannah was so nervous her stomach was upset and she was perspiring despite the cool weather. If there hadn't been so much construction noise outside she would have rolled down a window to get some fresh air. One thing about all that racket, she reasoned, fake workers wouldn't have bothered bringing in so much heavy equipment.

Finally, they were motioned to proceed

via a temporary detour. One short section of the road was so narrow Hannah held her breath and marveled at her grandmother's driving prowess.

She glanced back. Two more passenger cars had made it through. The semitruck behind them, however, seemed to be teetering.

"Oh, no. Is he…?"

Rafe whipped around. Lucy checked her mirrors. They both made unintelligible noises.

As their SUV put more distance between it and the detour, Hannah saw the semi slow, then stop. Something was definitely wrong.

"Is he off the road?" Lucy asked.

Hannah got on her knees to peer out the rear window. "I can't tell from here. Looks like it."

Still on the phone with the strike team leader, Rafe filled him in. "That's right. Looks like the bridge is going to be impassable until they manage to tow that eighteen-wheeler out of the way."

He paused, listening to the phone. All Hannah could hear was the thumping of her own heart in her ears.

"Yes, we're across," Rafe reported. He listened again, then looked at Lucy. Hannah didn't have to see his face to know he was concerned when he said, "No, it looked like a real accident," then added, "How long will that take?"

Finishing the call, Rafe explained. "There was roadwork scheduled for that bridge this week. I don't know if the accident was planned but seems too convenient to suit me. The rest of the strike team will either have to drive a hundred miles around or be brought to Gabaret by boat or chopper. All that takes time. They'll also attract attention if they approach by air."

Hannah's mind was racing, filled with endless questions and possible answers, none of which satisfied. "Wait. If they can't get onto the island, then Fleming won't be able to get off, right?"

Judging by the quick exchange of looks

between Rafe and Lucy, they didn't see it her way so Hannah asked, "What?"

"If they're the ones who blocked the bridge then it stands to reason they've prepared an alternate escape route."

"It won't matter as long as he can't get the victims out of the country. Police are watching the airfields, right?"

"At least the one his private plane always uses," Rafe said. "I hope it's not a decoy."

Hannah struggled to process the notion of all the innocent young people whose futures would be ruined if they weren't rescued. She looked to her companions. "Gram, Rafe, what are we going to do? We can't let this happen. We have to stop him."

Neither offered answers. Nor did Hannah have any. There were too many unknowns, too many ways the assault on the old hotel could go wrong. Too many ways even the cleverest plans could fail, she admitted with regret and more than a little fear. It was no good acting the part of a Trojan horse during a siege if there were no troops waiting to surprise the enemy and turn the tide of battle. Only a fool would walk into Deuce Fleming's hideout with no way to survive, let alone escape. She had intended to assist law enforcement, not replace it.

"This island hasn't been mapped for GPS," Lucy said. "Aerial views show a small settlement close to the southern tip. That's where we're heading."

"The whole place looks deserted."

"Not totally," Rafe warned, his voice raspy. His cell phone vibrated. He answered.

Hannah wasn't able to make out what was being said to him. However, his stricken expression told her he was receiving dire news. "Yes, sir. I understand."

He lowered the phone but didn't speak so Hannah did. "What? What's wrong?"

"Plenty," Rafe said.

"Well?"

"Our people on the east side of the river have reported unusual criminal activity. They're assembling another assault force over there but they won't be ready to move in on the hotel for at least three more hours."

Puzzled, she recalled the information they'd been given earlier. "That's still okay. Fleming isn't going to leave until tomorrow, right?"

Rafe was shaking his head. "No." He pocketed the phone, reached for his gun and rechecked the ammunition, chambering a live round the way he'd shown Hannah. "I was just told he's changed his plans at the last minute. They're set to fly out tonight as soon as it gets dark."

"How can you be sure this new information is correct?"

It was not a bit comforting to hear Rafe admit, "I can't."

EIGHTEEN

Ramshackle farm buildings sat grouped beside fallow fields as if their caretakers had been gone for generations. Roads were pitted and covered with fine, sandy dirt making them appear unpaved. If it had not recently rained to dampen the dust Rafe knew they'd be announcing their approach with every revolution of the tires. Not that it looked as if anyone would be able to sneak up on the old hotel no matter which direction they came from or what conveyance they chose to use.

"Fleming wasn't as dumb as I'd thought when he chose to stage here," Rafe said, assessing the landscape. "He's bound to spot us and anyone else long before we arrive."

"It'll take too long to park and walk in,"

Lucy said. She handed him an aerial view printed on copy paper. "I propose we drive to the built-up area you can see here and let Hannah out so she has a place to hide until backup finally shows."

Rafe knew what Hannah's reaction was going to be before she spoke and he wasn't disappointed. "I'm not hiding, okay? We're in this together."

"We were, before everything fell apart." Lucy slowed and pulled off the road, letting the SUV idle. "Things have changed."

"For the worse," Rafe added. "Your grandmother is right. You need to sit this one out."

Hannah made a face showing her disapproval. "Not happening."

"Too bad I didn't bring handcuffs," Lucy muttered.

"I can't believe you'd even consider cuffing me when I may need to defend myself." As she spoke, Hannah was rolling her eyes. "I'd be a sitting duck."

"You think you won't be if you try to approach the hotel with us?" He hated using such a derogatory tone but saw it as the lesser of two evils. The best thing Hannah could do for him and Lucy was back off so they didn't have to worry about her safety. Unfortunately, it didn't look as if she intended to comply.

"Let me get this straight," Hannah said. "You two plan to drive up to this derelict hotel where we know the Fleming gang is hanging out and just march into the lobby in the hope you can do something to keep him there until reinforcements arrive? That sounds way riskier than anything I might do."

"I suppose you have a better idea?"

"Not yet, but I have high hopes." She patted Lucy's shoulder. "Let's get going while we still have daylight. If Deuce really does plan to hit the road after sunset today we don't have much time left."

"I don't want to do something to set him off and make him start eliminating witnesses," Rafe warned. "We need to be very cautious."

"Assuming we can get close without being

seen," Lucy said. "I have a bad feeling that won't be easy."

"Well, three people and one dog can't successfully storm the place, that's for sure," Hannah countered. "Until backup arrives there's no way we can cut them off or keep them from loading the victims and taking off with them. If there were a dozen of us, we'd probably still be outgunned."

Cautious and loathe to encourage her, Rafe tilted his head to one side. "What do *you* think we should do to stall his leaving?"

"I prefer to show you rather than tell you," Hannah said.

Hair on the nape of Rafe's neck prickled and he suppressed a shiver. He didn't know what Hannah was up to. He didn't have to know. What he must do, however, was stop her from getting hurt or putting herself into an untenable position in regard to Fleming himself. They already knew the man had a score to settle with her.

"As long as it doesn't include you getting

yourself shot," Rafe gibed, hoping to lift the somber, confrontational mood with irony.

"Back atcha, mister," Hannah said. "It's my fondest wish that we all get to go home."

"Together," he said just above a whisper, not surprised when both women echoed, "Amen."

The grounds of the stone-built, turn-of-the-twentieth-century hotel were overgrown with wild vegetation and weeds. If Hannah had not known Deuce and his gang were inside she would never have guessed that anyone was, which was undoubtedly his plan when he chose the old building as his temporary headquarters.

Hannah lagged back after Lucy parked behind the remains of an old carriage house and everyone climbed out. Their black clothing would be a help once night fell, but right now it was unfortunately quite noticeable against the pale gray landscape. Only Thor blended in and even he had too much black accenting his brownish coat.

From her vantage point Hannah could see portions of the roof of the three-story hotel building. It didn't take binoculars to spot the armed sentries. Their silhouettes stood out against the cloudy sky.

Gram waved a signal for her to stay put while she and Rafe separated to approach from opposite directions. Hannah could already tell that the guards on the roof knew they were there because several of them were on the move, ostensibly to provide better protection against a ground assault.

Hannah saw only one way to stop the riflemen from firing on her companions. She needed Fleming's people to know who was there so they'd underestimate the threat. Underestimate her, specifically, just as Deuce had done during the prison escape.

Memories of movies where foolish heroines walked unarmed into dark houses or alleys flashed into her mind and almost made her smile. Many times she'd seen that happen and had judged those woman as beyond foolish. Now she could identify with them enough to start to understand.

Saying, "Thor, heel," she raised her hands above her head and stepped out where the sentries could see her.

When no one shot at her, she began to walk steadily toward the front doors of the hotel.

In the distance someone shouted, "No!"

Hannah kept going.

A lobby door swung open. She and Thor passed through. There was no going back now.

Running along behind the carriage house, Rafe rejoined Lucy. "Did you see that?"

"Yes." The older woman looked stricken. "I thought she had better sense."

"So did I or I would have tied her up."

"She'd have escaped anyway," Lucy said. "At least they didn't shoot at her when she showed herself."

"Small favors." Rafe was beside himself. He pulled out his phone, saw only one tiny bar of connection and used it anyway. Thankfully, he got through to the task force leader and was able to report the latest developments.

"Gutsy of her," the agent replied. "She's wearing the wire?"

"No," Rafe said. "We put it on the dog."

"Smart." He paused. "All right. Keep listening and relay anything pertinent ASAP."

"How is the accident on the bridge coming along?"

"A wrecker's on scene but there's so little room to maneuver on the detour he's having trouble clearing the road."

"Are your units ready to roll?"

"As soon as we can."

"Copy that." Rafe heard an odd thumping sound and looked to Lucy. She was pointing at the sky so he asked, "Did you send a chopper?"

"No. Why?"

"Because we see one circling to land in a field behind the hotel. I have a feeling our escaped felon is about to try to make his move."

"Do whatever you need to to stop him,"

the supervisor ordered. "Don't let him get away."

"Copy that," Rafe replied. He ended the call and focused on Lucy. "Any ideas?"

"Yes," she said. "I'm going to cause a diversion and you're going to get inside that hotel to rescue my granddaughter."

It occurred to Rafe that his chances of success were slim to none, yet he nodded agreement. Not only were there kidnap victims to free, he now had an unbelievably brave dog trainer to save, too. By himself.

He grabbed Lucy's arm to stop her and get her attention. "Tell me the plan."

Pointing, she explained. "As soon as that helicopter touches down and I hear the rotors slowing I'm going to drive this SUV right at it. If I time it right I'll be able to disable the chopper so Fleming can't use it. The trick will be to wait long enough that the pilot can't lift off and dodge but not so long that gang members are in place to provide covering fire."

"That might work."

"It has to," Lucy replied. "I'll try to give

you time to circle around and come in from the opposite side, but I won't wait too long. We'll only have one shot at this."

Rafe knew she was right. He also knew she was risking her life. They all were. Hannah was inside, Lucy was about to ram a helicopter with her armored SUV and he was charged with gaining covert access to a well-guarded fortress when no trooper in his right mind would try it.

Perhaps that was why the plan might work, he reasoned. Anything so off-the-wall would be unexpected.

The helicopter hovered, then slowly settled to the ground.

Lucy revved the engine and broke cover.

Rafe heard shouting and saw guards on the roof running east toward the wall facing the landing site.

A Jeep on the ground appeared out of nowhere and headed in the same direction, clearly racing to cut off the SUV attack.

Chancing an open run toward the front door Hannah had used, Rafe took the stone steps two at a time and burst into the lobby, gun drawn and ready to fire.

It was deserted.

Deuce Fleming's grin gave Hannah chills the moment she was delivered into his presence. Standing tall, she faced him with Thor at her side.

"What a nice surprise," he drawled. "Welcome."

"You won't escape this time," she said, thankful to note there was no tremor in her voice.

"We'll see." He motioned to one of his armed men. "Get rid of the dog."

"No!" She wrapped both arms around Thor's shoulders, using her body to block a potential bullet.

Fleming seemed amused. Laughing, he rescinded the order. "All right. Let her keep the cur for the present. We'll use him for target practice later when everybody can watch."

Hatred rose within Hannah to the point she was speechless. The commandment to love her enemies was impossible to keep when faced with the personification of evil that was Deuce Fleming.

Someone grabbed her arm and started to pull her away from Thor. Hannah screamed, resisting, and saw the loyal K-9 snap at the hand holding her.

"I'll come with you," she shouted. "Just don't hurt him. Please."

"Check her for a wire and lock them in with the others," Fleming ordered. "I'll personally deal with her later."

More than willing to submit to a search then follow one of the armed thugs down a hallway while a second trailed behind, Hannah kept Thor close and prayed he wouldn't try to bite unless she wanted him to. This was why he'd needed more training, more controlled practice, she thought, wishing there had been time to work with him. Having a basically untrained dog with the strength and protective instincts Thor possessed could be dangerous to everyone, even to her if he chose to cause trouble and she wasn't able to call him off.

The leader paused at wide polished oak doors and used a large key to unlock one of them. As it swung open, Hannah saw a stirring of individuals huddled in chairs and on blankets spread on the floor. As near as she could tell there were at least two dozen women, all young and all frightened.

No one spoke until the door shut behind her and its lock clicked. Then Hannah began to talk for the benefit of the listening device on Thor's harness. "This looks like a banquet or ballroom. Ground floor. There are lots of people here, maybe twenty-five or thirty."

Keeping her dog on a short leash she scanned the crowd. "Is one of you named Kristy Fellows?"

A hand was raised cautiously. "Me."

"Your father is a state trooper?"

Kristy quickly put down her hand and shook her head.

"It's okay," Hannah assured her. "I've met Andy. He's still in the hospital but recovering."

The teen remained visibly leery so Hannah changed her focus. "I want you all to know that the authorities are aware of your presence and are making plans for a rescue. We need to stay calm and wait."

"How long?" someone in the dim background asked. "Some of us have been prisoners here for weeks."

"That's better than the alternative," Hannah said. "Once you're shipped out of the country, it'll be too late."

"What are you doing in here with us?" another asked.

"Have you ever read the story of the Trojan horse?" Most of the women shook their heads. "Well, never mind. Just think of me as your guide to getting rescued, okay."

Crossing the room she began to investigate the tall windows hidden behind heavy drapes. There were, unfortunately, iron grids on the outside preventing escape.

"They're all like that," Kristy said, joining her.

"I take it the doors are pretty solid, too."

"Like a fortress," the slim young woman said. "Did you really see my dad?"

"Yes. His former partner took me."

"Gavin?"

"No," Hannah said before realizing that might be Rafe's real name. "Rafe McDowell."

Kristy made a face. "Never heard of him."

"Doesn't matter. I know it was your father I spoke with. He's on the mend and praying for you. Lots of people are."

"Yeah, well, I already tried that and I'm still here."

"Ah, but help is coming," Hannah reminded her. "That's a direct answer to a lot of prayers."

"Only if it happens," Kristy grumbled, eyeing the nervous German shepherd and Hannah. "So far I'm not real impressed."

"Give us time," Hannah countered. She smiled at Thor and spoke close to his harness to make sure her message was received. "As soon as my friends hear we're being held in a big room on the first floor with fancy iron bars over the tall windows, they'll know just how to break us out."

Kristy snorted in derision. "Right. And that dog is going to make like Lassie and go tell them."

"In a manner of speaking," Hannah said.

She led Thor to the center of the room and climbed up on a chair to be seen and heard by all. "I know you're scared. Me, too. But we have to be ready to move when help arrives. I can't tell you exactly how or when that will happen. All I know for sure is that there are lots of brave police officers and government agents working together to get us out of here."

A low murmur among the prisoners told her they were discussing the news and deciding whether or not to believe her. Mistrust was normal. After all, they'd been kidnapped and moved around for who knows how long. They were bound to be skeptical.

"Remember," Hannah told them, "I chose to walk into this place and join you. I believe we're all going to survive."

Which was true, as far as it went. The more she thought about what she'd done, however, the more she likened herself to one of those movie heroines who walked boldly into untenable situations. Her problem was that this was not a script with a guaranteed happy ending. This was real life.

NINETEEN

Once inside the hotel, Rafe kept to the periphery of the lobby, hugging the walls and darting from hiding place to hiding place as much as was possible. A tarnished, dusty chandelier hung from the high ceiling and yellowing sheets draped the upholstered furniture. Myriad footprints had disturbed the layer of dirt on the marble floor. To his relief, Thor's paws had also left their marks.

Rafe was about to break cover and circle the base of the spiral staircase to look for the room Hannah had described via the radio Thor carried. A rumble of voices stopped him. Crouching behind a settee he listened intently.

Someone muttered a curse. "He has to be out of his mind."

Another man answered. "Who cares as long as we're on his good side. Just don't make a mistake and you'll be fine."

"Mistakes? Deuce is the one making those. I can't believe he didn't shoot that woman and her dog the minute he saw them."

A shiver snaked up Rafe's spine and made the hair at the nape of his neck prickle. Any mention of a woman with a dog had to be Hannah and Thor. *They're still alive!*

"Didn't you hear what the boss said? He's saving them for later. There's nothin' like watchin' somebody get shot to make all the others behave better."

"Yeah, yeah, I know. It just seems dumb to put her in with our cargo, if you get my drift."

"She wasn't armed. She can't cause any trouble that we can't handle."

"What about the chopper. Somebody took that out."

"No sweat. The boss has another one coming. Boats, too. We'll be heading for warm, sandy beaches and palm trees by tonight. You'll see."

"Yeah, well, in the meantime, what're we supposed to do with the driver who messed up our getaway bird?"

"That was just some old lady. They're bringin' her in. Nothin' to worry about."

Every muscle in Rafe's body was taut, his heart racing, his stomach clenching almost as tightly as his fists. They had captured Lucy, which sounded good only because it meant she was also alive and presumably mobile. He waited, ready to intervene if necessary and praying he wouldn't have to show himself until he was in a better position to gain control.

Two other thugs appeared at the door, supporting the older woman between them. She was acting groggy and disoriented but Rafe suspected a ruse on her part. The gang had already written her off as being no threat. Continuing to act that way was definitely a ploy the former spy would use.

Assessing Lucy's condition as the trio passed, Rafe saw her eyes open briefly and scan the lobby. That was enough to reassure him she was faking. Chances were she hadn't made it out of the SUV with her gun, but at least he now had a second ally inside the hotel. Hopefully, she had relayed the information they'd heard over the radio to the main task force. When they finally arrived they'd need to know where the hostages were being kept and how big a force was needed to free them.

Deuce Fleming appeared at the top of the staircase and started down. He laughed. "Well, well, well, if it isn't Granny, herself. She's got more guts than I thought."

One of the men supporting her asked, "What you want we should do with her?"

"Throw her in with the others. It'll be a lesson to them."

Rafe could not have made a more advantageous choice if Fleming had consulted him. Putting Lucy and Hannah together was akin to mixing gasoline and matches. He was positive they would do whatever they could to delay the departure of the human trafficking victims until backup arrived. Lucy had begun active interference when she'd eliminated the first helicopter. No matter what came next, those two extraordinary women would hinder Fleming. Once the gang's escape plans were carried out and they were airborne, stopping them would be next to impossible.

Wild notions of Hannah and Lucy trying to hijack Fleming's plane gave Rafe the shivers. This operation must never be allowed to get that far. Not if he expected to save all those kidnap victims as well as the spunky former spy and the woman he… Rafe held his breath. The woman he what? Admired? Yes, and more…

Unwelcome feelings of both joy and dread filled him. Circumstances had apparently acted as a catalyst and had influenced him beyond belief. Like it or not, he was definitely falling in love with Hannah Lassiter. What a disaster.

Hannah had herded the others away from the doors and into a back corner of the ballroom, stationing herself and Thor between the victims and the door she had entered. When it opened again and someone shoved a small figure through, she knew at a glance who it was. The others, however, did not so they shrank back as the door slammed shut again. Some were weeping. Some acted so depressed Hannah wasn't sure she could motivate them enough to engineer a mass exodus.

"Gram!" Thor followed her as she ran to Lucy, fell to her knees and embraced her.

The older woman barely moved until she'd scanned the room. Then she took a shaky breath and pressed a hand to her ribs. "Help me up."

Leaning on Hannah's arm she gave a muffled groan, dusted off her dark clothing and cautiously stretched sore muscles before cracking a smile. "Feels worse than it looks."

"But you're okay?" Hannah asked.

"I will be. Don't worry. I relayed your info to the task force just before I took out the chopper."

"Good. I was hoping the bug was working. Now what?"

"Now, we wait."

Hannah scowled. "I'm not convinced we'll have enough time to get away if we're too passive."

"Why? What else have you heard?"

"Plenty. The plans to move out keep changing." She gestured at the group behind her. "They tell me the kidnappers have gotten so used to having them around they've started talking freely in front of them. Fleming plans to gather everyone at a private airfield where he has a chartered plane waiting. Exactly where that is keeps changing so they can't agree on that detail."

"What about timing? You say it's changing?" Lucy asked.

"Yes. We all thought he was going to leave tomorrow. Now, it's supposed to happen today."

"I take it the chopper was part of his escape plan."

"Yes." Hannah smiled. "He was so steamed

about what you did, they could hear him hollering through the walls."

"Good." She grinned briefly before sobering. "I worry that you're not taking this whole thing seriously enough. I've seen agents with too much confidence pay the ultimate price for that kind of blasé attitude. Don't make that mistake, Hannah. Life doesn't get more dangerous than this."

"I know that, in an academic way. Without the experience you and Rafe have had, it's really hard to believe any of this is actually happening to us." Gesturing at the prisoners, she shook her head pensively. "I mean, look at all of them. It's so sad to think about how many families are grieving."

"Did you locate Kristy?"

"Yes." Hannah pointed out a slim brunette standing off to the side and comforting a weeping blond teen. "That's her."

"She looks pretty levelheaded. Think we can count on her not falling apart in a crisis?"

"I do."

"What about you?" Lucy asked, eyebrows raised. "How are you feeling? Steady? Strong?"

"I thought you wanted me to be worried," Hannah said, half teasing, half serious. "Do you think Rafe is okay?"

"I do. These guys would be bragging if they'd taken him out."

"I guess that's comforting." She stroked Thor's broad forehead to help calm herself. Thinking about Rafe, worrying about his safety minute to minute, was bound to distract her and that wasn't good. Not good at all. Gram was right, though. If they had harmed Rafe they'd be celebrating the defeat of an enemy whether they knew he was a cop or not.

She considered warning Kristy to keep that information to herself, then recalled the gang member who had tried to shoot poor Andy in his hospital room. Fleming was smart. He must have figured out which side Rafe was on long ago. Truth to tell, there probably wasn't a lot that the clever criminal didn't know. What he chose to do with that info, how he might use it, was the only real unknown.

That, and how she and Gram were going to shepherd this sad bunch of victims to safety without setting off World War III. If she let herself look at the big picture and take everything into account, she'd have to admit their chances were poor. Except, the good guys in the white hats were supposed to win, weren't they? Wasn't that how such stories ended?

Trying to calm her turbulent thoughts and clear her head of unnecessary concerns, Hannah took a deep breath and released it slowly, then another. And another. By that time she had concluded that God would not have put her into such an untenable situation if He didn't intend to get her out of it.

"If His will is really how I got here," she murmured, recalling the poor decisions that had led to the jailbreak in the first place. Believers had free will. They could make all the mistakes they wanted in spite of prior commitments to their faith. Surrendering to Him didn't mean they would never face hardships. It did, however, promise that they would never have to do so alone. Forgiveness waited for anyone who asked for it, for anyone who realized they had done wrong and admitted it. *Even Deuce Fleming*, her heart suddenly insisted.

Hannah refused to listen. Surely there were some sins, some crimes, which were beyond forgiveness. Look at all the terrible suffering that man had caused and was still causing.

She was not about to forgive a man who had harmed so many innocents, ruined so many lives, and left hope shredded and trampled in his wake.

If evil had a face it was Deuce Fleming's.

Rafe was essentially trapped in the lobby. Fleming had gone back upstairs but his men kept coming and going, even posting an armed guard just outside the front door. He shifted as he crouched to keep up circulation in his legs. Ambient noise as the gang prepared to travel was to his advantage. Knowing how close they were to leaving, however, was more than unsettling. It was terrifying.

He'd overheard plans vital to an effective capture and would gladly have relayed them to the task force if he'd been alone. Stuck in the cavernous lobby he didn't dare make any noise, let alone carry on a phone or radio conversation.

Seeing the door guard turn his back and pace away, Rafe decided to take a chance on changing positions. Nobody was currently on the stairs and he didn't see other gang members loitering around the lobby at the moment so he slowly straightened, bracing himself on the back of the settee. He listened. There was muted conversation in the distance but nothing sounded close by.

Moving toward the rear of the room he ducked beneath the sweeping staircase. Beams of pink and orange sunlight filled with swirling dust particles cut across his path, reminding him of how little time he had left before night came.

Thanks to Lucy's capture, he knew the prisoners were confined behind the double doors to his right. To his left lay an open corridor. He chose the latter, hoping and praying it would give him enough cover to safely report to the strike team by phone. Once he had done that and had learned how long it might be before backup arrived, he'd decide what to do about freeing the prisoners. About rescuing Hannah and the rest.

An acrid smell gave him pause. *Gasoline?* Yes, Rafe concluded. There was no reason for that to be kept inside, yet there was no doubt about the odor.

Following the fumes he opened a door marked Janitor, intending to duck out of sight and make his phone call. The smell became overwhelming. He looked down. Rows of gasoline-filled bottles had been rigged with wicks sticking out their necks, ready to be lit and thrown as weapons. He frowned. These men had plenty of armament. They didn't need Molotov cocktails to defend themselves. So what were they planning to do with them? The only conclusion he could come to was to anticipate the total destruction of the old hotel by fire.

Coughing from the fumes in the closet he pulled out his phone, made the connection and began to report. "Yes, Colonel. That's right. It looks as though they intend to set fire to this place when they leave. How long before you get here?"

"The bridge is clearing as we speak. Some of my people started the drive around so I don't have a full team but we're also pulling units from the Illinois side of the river."

"What's your ETA?"

"I should arrive within the next ninety minutes. We'll stage away from the hotel until we have enough firepower to take the place by overwhelming force."

Rafe felt sick. "A siege isn't going to protect the hostages. If anything, it'll get them killed."

"I'll try to talk Fleming down first. We've already cut off escape by land and I'm working on blockading the river."

"There's still the air to think about," Rafe warned. "I told you what happened to the first chopper they brought in. I've since heard that they've got more than one. With all the flat fields around here they won't have trouble finding a new place to land."

"We'll use drones to reconnoiter once we're in position. Do what you can on your end to keep them from being shot down."

"Copy." He coughed more, smothering the sound with his sleeve. "I'll try to check in again if I can find a secluded spot to call from. If you don't hear from me, that won't mean I'm out of commission, okay? According to what I've been hearing, the women and the dog are locked up with the other prisoners. I'm going to do my best to get them out of here before it's too late."

"Just don't get yourself killed, Gavin."

It seemed odd to hear his real name spoken when he'd been called Rafe for so long. Nevertheless, it was strangely comforting to hear his boss refer to him that way.

"From your lips to God's ears," he said, repeating a saying he'd heard Hannah use as he ended the conversation. That led him to add, "Please, Father. Help me help her and all of them."

Resolved, he opened the closet door, checked the hallway and started out.

He'd barely gone ten paces when he turned back, reentered the closet and tipped every bottle on its side. It wasn't much but who knew? It might actually help.

TWENTY

As far as Hannah was concerned, as long as the heavy doors stayed closed they protected as much as hindered. Since Gram had arrived so unceremoniously, she'd kept insisting she felt fine. Hannah was not so sure. She didn't like the older woman's pale color or the perspiration glistening on her forehead when the room was anything but hot.

"Just let me catch my breath for a few seconds," Lucy said. "Then we'll figure out how to escape."

"We could wait for rescue," Hannah told her. "The bridge must be clear by now."

"Right, I…" Lucy's voice faded to nothing. She closed her eyes and slumped in the chair.

Hannah caught her before she could slip to the floor. Kristy helped her lower the older woman onto a blanket on the floor. "What's wrong with her?" the teen asked.

"I don't know. It could be anything. She drove our SUV into the helicopter. I thought she was faking being out of it when they brought her in, but maybe she really was injured."

"I'm so sorry," Kristy said. "How can I help?"

Normally, Hannah would have deferred to her grandmother. Now that wasn't an option. She checked Lucy's pulse and found it strong, watched her breathing and judged it even enough for now. If she hadn't seen Gram faint moments ago, she'd have thought she was merely sleeping. She knew enough about human medicine to alleviate serious worry, at least for the present, although broken ribs were a worrisome possibility.

"Okay," Hannah said. "Here's what I know and what I don't. I came here with Gram and one other person, the man who calls himself Rafe McDowell. He said he was your dad's state trooper partner and he's been helping us track Fleming ever since the jailbreak."

"I heard them talking about that," Kristy said in a near whisper. "That was you with the dog?"

"Yes. Thor," Hannah replied, causing the K-9 to lean against her even more.

Kristy fell to her knees next to the German shepherd and hugged him as if he were a big stuffed toy. That Thor let her do so was something of a surprise to Hannah. Soothing the dog with a "Good boy," she touched the girl's slim shoulder through her shirt. "You should never hug a strange dog like that."

"He's a sweetie. I can tell."

"Sometimes," Hannah said. "He's been known to bite the bad guys."

"Smart, too, huh?"

That made Hannah smile. "Yes, but untrained. Always keep that in mind. He's protective but not predictable."

Seeing Thor duck out of the girl's embrace and turn to the blanket where Lucy lay, Hannah was relieved to see her grandmother had regained consciousness so she knelt next to her. "How are you feeling?"

"Good enough to get out of here." Lucy raised on one elbow and grimaced. "Ouch."

"Stay down and rest a bit more," Hannah said. "Kristy and I are going to scout around for an escape route."

Lucy glanced at the heavy brocade drapes. "Can't we break a window?"

"They're barred," the girl said.

"Then we'll find some other way," Hannah said flatly. She touched the older woman's shoulder. "You stay put and just use your brain to figure things out. We'll walk around and investigate."

"I can come with you."

"And keep me from concentrating on my job because I'm too worried about your health? I don't think so." This was the first time in recent memory she had overtly disagreed with her wise grandmother and refused to consider doing everything her way. In Hannah's mind it was less a matter of independence than it was of respect. As long as Lucy was at her best Hannah was perfectly willing to defer to her opinions. Now, however, things were different.

The expression on Lucy's face was a combination of surprise and disagreement so Hannah restated her decision. "You know I love you, Gram. I do. But I'm right this time and you know it."

"Okay, okay." Lowering herself all the way, Lucy tucked part of the blanket beneath her head as a makeshift pillow. "Go explore without me. Just don't do anything rash."

Relieved to be able to carry on a lucid conversation with the sweet lady who had practically raised her, Hannah managed a smile. "What, like helping felons escape from prison, you mean?"

"Yeah, something like that." Lucy returned the smile.

Standing beside Hannah, Kristy grabbed her arm. "Wait a second. You got Fleming out of jail?"

"It's a long story," Hannah told her. "One

for another time. Right now, you and I need to check this room for some way out."

"There isn't any. We looked." She gestured at her fellow kidnap victims. "All of us did."

"I'm sure you did. Now we'll see what the dog can tell us."

In reality, Hannah wasn't expecting much. She already knew the heavy doors were locked and the windows barred. Still, as she'd just told Kristy, it wouldn't hurt to look again.

Leading the shepherd to the wall on her left, she walked slowly along it, came to the rear corner and made a turn. The walls looked solid. Impenetrable. When Fleming had chosen to lock his victims in the ballroom, or whatever it had originally been, he'd chosen wisely.

There was one thing she was thankful for, the view through the tall windows. Checking each one as she passed, she noted the wrecked SUV embedded in the lower part of the helicopter tail section. No way was that bird going to fly anytime soon.

A dusty, camo-painted Jeep was slowly circling the building. She ducked behind the curtain to keep the driver from noticing her. If Rafe could steal that and wrap a chain around the grid on one of the windows he might be able to pull it off and let them escape that way, except what would they do about Fleming's armed men? she asked herself. And what good would it be to get out of the hotel with nowhere to go, no place to hide?

Most of all, Hannah wished she knew how much longer it was going to be before the force she'd seen preparing to attack actually got there. Not knowing that crucial detail meant they didn't dare leave the hotel. They'd be sitting ducks out in those flat, treeless fields.

It occurred to her that escape from that room was only the beginning. Once she'd gotten all the kidnap victims out, what was she going to do with them? And how much cooperation could she expect if and when they were free?

Pulled from her whirling thoughts by

Thor's tug on the leash, Hannah frowned. He was pawing at the base of an ornately carved credenza. She signaled Kristy. "Come help me push this."

Although the teen asked why, she nevertheless put her shoulder to the heavy piece of furniture and shoved.

Dust swirled. A mouse darted out. Thor ignored it, continuing to dig at the narrow space between the cabinet and the wall.

It wasn't necessary to completely displace the furniture in order to see the waist-high, built-in pass-through. It had obviously been closed off long ago.

Hannah dropped the leash, worked her fingertips into a gap between the small door and jamb, then yanked. It took her three tries before it budged. By this time, some of the other victims had joined her.

"Back off. Everybody. Give me room."

Eager hands pushed and pulled the credenza until the small access to the opening was clear. Hannah paused, waved both hands and shushed them. "Quiet down before somebody hears you and comes to see why you're so excited."

She opened the door to the passage and saw a similar one barring the way on the other side. If there was another piece of heavy furniture barring that door, they'd never manage to push hard enough to move it.

Turning to address the prisoners, she waited for complete quiet. "Listen carefully. I have no way of knowing who or what is on the other side of this hole. I did see a diagram of the hotel when we met with members of your rescue team and I think there's a kitchen through there. If so, there may be a bunch of men using it right now."

A murmur went through the group.

"It might make noise when I try to open it and that may bring guards to check on us." She had an idea. "Get a couple of those blankets and drape them over me to muffle the sound, just in case."

As soon as her plans were in place she gave the door a push. Nothing happened.

"Okay, it's really stuck. A few of you

stand close and support me so I can lean back and try to kick it open."

Ranks closed behind Hannah. She rested against helpful hands and arms to literally walk her feet up the wall, planted the left one and kicked with the right. The jamb splintered. The little door swung open so hard it hammered the wall then vibrated to a stop.

Hannah jumped down to peer through. As she had hoped and prayed there was an empty room on the opposite side. They had a way out!

The blankets fell away. Someone cheered softly while some wept and hugged each other. Only Hannah seemed to realize they weren't in the clear. Far from it. Once she had moved all the prisoners out of their temporary prison they still had nowhere safe to go. Not until the task force arrived.

Joy mixed with trepidation brought unshed tears to her eyes, too. Seeing her grandmother at the rear of the group, silently clapping her hands, was enough to make the tears fall. She dashed them away and climbed up on a chair to stand where they could all see and hear her.

"This is just the beginning," Hannah said. "If we run outside we're bound to be recaptured. We have to be smart. Smarter than the gang that put us here."

A low rumble filled the room, causing Hannah to pause her instructions. "Listen. Listen."

Eager faces were upturned, watching her intently. "Here's what we need to do. This is a big hotel and I doubt they've opened many guest rooms because they don't need them. It will be up to us to find those empty spaces and hide ourselves until we hear the police arriving. They are coming, I'm just not sure how soon. Above all, we need to keep from being transported somewhere else. That's the key to survival and rescue. Understand?"

She saw nods spreading through the group. "All right. Who's first?"

From the rear, Lucy's voice rose over the ambient noise. "Send the dog and then you follow him to defend us when we get there."

That made Hannah smile. So did Kristy's comment. "I see who you inherited your brains from."

"Right," Hannah said. She lifted Thor's head and shoulders to face the opening. Kristy boosted from the rear. As soon as he landed and Hannah saw he was waiting for her, she stood on tiptoe and wriggled through.

"I recommend coming feet first," she called quietly back to the others. "Unless you want to land on your heads."

As she stepped back, arms out and ready to assist the next young woman to pass through, it occurred to her that she might have just put them all in worse jeopardy so she began to pray.

"Thank You, Father, for providing this chance. Please continue to protect and guide us. Guide me."

Hannah had to believe God was on her side and had placed her with the prisoners in order to help them, because if she was wrong about divine guidance she could very well be making a grievous error.

That thought made her tremble. If they were caught again it was possible Deuce Fleming would keep his promise to shoot Thor and probably her, too.

The urge to turn and flee, to run from the duty she had accepted regarding everyone else, was so strong it made her weak-kneed. It also brought unfounded guilt for merely considering abandoning them. Of course she was staying. There was no doubt of it.

Considering her past life in comparison to an unsure future, she had only one regret. That she hadn't spoken up when she'd had the chance and told Rafe McDowell how fond of him she had grown. Now he was out there somewhere, risking his own life for all of them.

"Please, Lord, let me see him again," Hannah added to her ongoing prayers, promising herself she'd confess everything she felt for him. The only question left to ask was, why had she grown to care so deeply for that man when she didn't even know his real name.

TWENTY-ONE

Working his way through the hotel on the main floor, Rafe managed to keep from being spotted. The last he'd seen of Fleming he'd been climbing the staircase, meaning he was likely still upstairs.

It occurred to Rafe that if he could actually capture the leader, the gang might surrender. Then again, they might not. Plus, he had Hannah and Lucy to worry about besides the original hostages. One man with one gun, namely himself, was not going to be able to control everybody. Period. He might be good, actually he was very good, but that didn't make him omnipotent. Only God was that and judging by their present predicament, Rafe wasn't convinced He was paying enough attention.

Looking back on the trials he and Hannah had shared, he did have to admit something awesome was happening. When she'd broadcast Kristy's name over and over, as if they were already friends, he'd felt an enormous relief. A burden had accompanied that, of course. Now he knew for sure that Andy's daughter was among the prisoners, meaning there was no margin for error. Truth to tell, there never was when he was on the job, even if a few mistakes did sneak past him from time to time.

The key to being fearless in the face of danger was total self-confidence. Doubting himself even a little was not a good sign. Not good at all. And doubting the sovereignty of God? *Worse.* Way worse. Rafe closed his eyes and sent up a silent prayer for forgiveness. For strength of body and character. And for the innocent victims he and those in his profession had not been able to save in the past. Their numbers had to be staggering.

He had earlier muted the Bluetooth-like radio receiver stuck in his ear. Now that he was away from anyone else and able to listen without risk of being detected he reactivated the sound. Instead of the conversation he'd heard before there was shuffling and grunting and panting. Whispers were distorted by background noise. Oh, how he wished the connection was two-way so he could ask what was going on.

Breaking cover, he headed for the core of the hotel, the central ballroom. That was where Hannah had reported being held with the kidnap victims and that was where he'd seen them put Lucy. Since he had not heard or seen any mass movement of gang members or prisoners, they had to still be in there. What he'd do when and if he reached them was an unanswered question.

As he peered around a corner into a section of the lobby he noticed two armed men; a bulky one with a military buzz cut and another, shorter and slimmer, with a head of brown curls. They each had an ear pressed to massive oak doors and were arguing.

"I tell ya, I heard something," Curls said.

"Yeah, yeah. You're always hearing stuff that ain't there."

"We need to have a look."

"Well, I'm not unlockin' this door. If you want to do it and the boss blows a gasket, it's all on you."

Rafe watched Buzz Cut hand an ornate large antique key to his partner and back away. Curly holstered his gun then bent over the lock, apparently having trouble inserting the key.

"If I'd known you were gonna shake so bad I'd of done that myself," the larger man said. "Hurry it up, will ya?"

Yes, please, Rafe thought. As soon as they opened that door he would know Hannah and Lucy and the others were all right and could proceed to locate Deuce so he'd be in position to detain him when the strike team was about to arrive. Forcing him to call off his men wasn't the best plan Rafe had ever had, but given the situation he saw no alternatives.

Cursing, the short-haired thug shoved his own sidearm into its holster and wrested the key away. Unlocking the door he gave it a hard push, shouted to the slimmer man and they both disappeared through the doorway.

Rafe paused only a millisecond before sprinting across the lobby to the same door. Neither gang member noticed his entry. They were too busy fighting over which one was going to crawl through a small opening in a far wall.

The enormous room was empty except for the three of them.

"Hands in the air," Rafe shouted. "Now."

Buzz Cut started to go for his gun, then froze when he turned and saw Rafe pointing the Glock at him. Curls raised his hands first.

"On the floor," Rafe ordered. "Both of you. Face down." Crossing quickly he disarmed both men then used the handcuffs they were carrying to lock them in place, back-to-back. "You have the choice to keep quiet on your own or be knocked out." He displayed the grip of one of the guns he'd taken off them. "Which will it be?"

"I'm not sayin' a word," Curly immediately offered.

His companion agreed with a grimace and a nod. "Yeah, yeah."

"Okay. I'll come back and see that neither of you ever talks again if you break your promise. Got that?"

"I said so, didn't I? The boss is liable to do it for you if he thinks we let his merchandise get away."

"That's your problem," Rafe said. "I'll send somebody back for you once everything is under control." He took a moment to look through the hole in the wall, saw nothing but a white-painted board blocking the other side, and tried to push it open. Since it didn't budge he figured it was locked and left it as he'd found it.

"Who are you, anyway?" one of the men asked.

"Your worst enemy," Rafe told him.

"Naw," Buzz Cut argued. "Our worst enemy is Deuce Fleming."

Enjoying his unexpected success Rafe

cracked a smile. "Funny you should say that. He's mine, too."

Leaving them prostrate on the bare floor, Rafe gathered up their guns and started away.

"Hey. Where are you going?"

"Don't worry, boys. I'll lock you in and keep the key so you'll be safe enough until this is all over."

And just like that there were two less adversaries to worry about when the siege began, he mused, locking the room and pocketing the heavy brass key.

Stepping into a small alcove for privacy he opened his cell phone to check the schematics of the hotel that they'd been given. A kitchen and prep area lay on the other side of the opening he'd seen. Clearly, Hannah had found a way out and taken the other captives with her. For once he wished she hadn't been clever enough to secure the second little door after passing through.

Then again, nothing indicated that she'd stayed where she'd landed. She was too smart for that. No, she'd have led the victims to someplace she felt was safe, meaning it was highly unlikely they were still gathered in the kitchen.

Nevertheless, he circled to one of the rear accesses and checked. Dust coated every surface except one section of stainless steel counter. That area showed overlapping foot and hand prints with places where bodies had landed and slid off. Rafe was elated. Hannah had done it. She'd freed the others just as he'd hoped and led them away. Good for her.

He was turning to leave to search for them when he decided to pause long enough to disturb the dust in other places and use a dry mop to obliterate any footprints on the dusty floor. If he could tell which way the group had gone, then so could Fleming's cohorts.

By the time Rafe was finished, he'd left false trails to both outside exits and had swept the interior hallway. Then he backed away, dragging the dry mop behind him so whoever discovered his tracks wouldn't be able to tell if he was coming or going.

Satisfied, he stuffed the mop into the janitor's closet with the spilled gasoline and went looking for the victims. Pride in Hannah made him smile in spite of the tenuous situation. Intel had shown that the kidnapped women had been held at the hotel for days, yet it took Hannah Lassiter to find a way for them to escape. What an amazing person she was. When all this was over he was going to make sure she was recognized for her heroism.

Fond thoughts carried him further and he imagined being the one chosen to pin a medal on her or hand her a certificate for exceptional valor. His heart swelled with pride and affection. Awareness grew. If she had merely been lovely, as she certainly was, she would have been appealing. Knowing how brave and clever she was had taken his admiration to another level. He'd met and even dated pretty women in the past, yet none of them had impressed him this much. None had made his head spin and his heart race the way thinking of Hannah did.

Rafe paused, listening to his earpiece and wondering why everything seemed quiet. The next words he heard were so softly spoken he had to strain to make them out.

"Gram? Gram, can you make it?"

Whatever the answer was, the tiny radio pinned on Thor didn't pick it up. Thankfully, he could hear Hannah say, "Come on. We'll help you." Then a pause and, "Hurry."

Where were they? Had they left the building? Were they still inside, and if so, where?

The schematics on his cell phone showed the main staircase where he'd last seen Deuce. Looking carefully at details of the kitchen area he noted a narrow, closed-off stairway meant for staff use. If he was Hannah, that's how he'd have left the kitchen. The problem was, once she and the others reached the upper floors they were likely to run into Fleming and the men in his closest circle.

Rafe reentered the kitchen and easily located the simple stairs behind a door. He wasn't picking up sounds of movement ahead, but the disturbed dust on the worn, wooden steps was a strong clue. Not only were there shoe prints, the paws of a large canine had left clear marks along one edge. They were up there. And, if they weren't careful, they'd stumble onto their captors.

Moving as silently as possible, Rafe was about to start his climb when he thought he heard something in the distance. *Sirens.* He pulled out his cell phone and tried to call his superintendent. *No service.*

At his wit's end, Rafe took the stairs two at a time, paused at the door at the top to draw his gun, then eased it open and peered out.

There was no sign of Hannah, but armed men were running past. In the background, Fleming was shouting orders that sounded as though he was dispersing troops to defend a fort.

Anxious to find Hannah and the other prisoners, Rafe held himself back until the hallways emptied. Then he slowly counted to ten and eased the door open for a better look. All was quiet. He couldn't have cleared the second floor more efficiently if he'd tried.

"Speaking of answered prayer..." He cast his eyes upward. "Thank You, Father. Now where are the women?"

Lacking a clear answer he turned right, away from the stairs, and made his way to the corner at the far end of the hallway. More closed rooms lay ahead. What he wanted to do was bang on each door in turn until Hannah showed herself. He would have if caution hadn't been called for. Suppose all of Fleming's men had not descended to the lobby. It would only take one sounding an alarm to spoil any chances Rafe had of getting to the prisoners and guiding them to safety.

His cell phone vibrated in his pocket. "Hello?"

"Situation report," his supervisor said without wasting time on polite conversation.

"The hostages have escaped and are at large in the hotel," Rafe reported. "Fleming may not know they're gone yet. Right now he's acting more worried about how many of our units are closing in. I know he's posted snipers on the roof and probably other places, too. Tell our people to assume everyone is armed and dangerous."

"Copy that. Where are you?"

"At the moment, on the second floor. If I don't locate the victims here, I'll go on up to three."

"Advise when you have them and we'll give you cover as best we can."

"I think we should hold off trying to move anybody until you have the gang disarmed. We'll have casualties if we don't."

"Copy."

Rafe heard him broadcasting to the cars making their approach. Sirens wailed louder, closer. He opened one of the first rooms he came to and hurried to the window. The glass was barely clean enough to see through but flashing red and blue lights helped him tell what was transpiring in the twilight below.

Someone fired the first shot. A volley of gunfire ensued. Rafe ducked just in case a stray bullet came his way. Men on the floor below were shouting and cursing. Deuce Fleming's voice rose over the din. "Go get the women. We'll use them as human shields."

Rafe held his breath. As soon as they discovered their prisoners had escaped they'd begin a frantic search. There would be no place to hide. Not with a dozen armed thugs searching for them.

He fisted his phone again. "They're about to find out the victims aren't locked up where they left them. I'll make a stand at the top of the main staircase but I don't know how long I can hold them off."

"Do your best," his superintendent said. "We'll make entry ASAP, but I can't guarantee how soon that will be."

There was nothing more to say. Rafe took up a defensive position at the corner facing the top of the stairs, laid out the extra guns he'd taken from the men he'd overpowered in the ballroom and waited, knowing he might be living his last moments on earth.

The urge to pray was strong but he had

no words, no sensible pleas, not even a remembered verse from his childhood.

That doesn't matter, he thought soberly. It didn't take flowery words or complicated prayers to reach out to God. A simple, heartfelt "Jesus," was more than enough. So that's exactly what he whispered. Over and over.

TWENTY-TWO

Hannah had shepherded her group as far as they could go without actually stepping out onto the roof. She knew there had been snipers up there before and likely still were so she chose a room at the farthest point away from that access. The plan wasn't foolproof. Nothing could be under such desperate circumstances. But anything was better than staying locked in that ballroom and waiting for their captors to come for them.

It had occurred to her more than once that she could have remained outside when they'd arrived at the hotel. Maybe it was foolish to have offered herself as another victim, but she still couldn't see any other feasible way to contact these poor girls and let them know help was on the way. Plus, she and Thor had managed to free them from that room where they'd been held, providing an added buffer against the explosive temper of Deuce Fleming. If he acted impulsively as he had before and decided to shoot them or use them to facilitate his own escape, he'd have to find them first. And that would take time, time he might not have once the police assault on his hideout began in earnest.

The hotel room smelled musty and was even dirtier than the common areas. Several of the women chose to sit on the edge of the bare mattress, but many preferred to stand. Lucy stood at one of the windows peering out through slits in the vertical blinds.

"What do you see?" Hannah asked.

"A full-on assault," her grandmother answered. "The command van we saw before just pulled behind the carriage house where I parked. Police cars are driving around this building. I can't see them all but it reminds me of a siege. It looks like Fleming is trapped."

"Perfect."

"I'll feel better once they've made entry and taken the gang into custody."

"It shouldn't take long. Deuce is going to be furious when he opens the ballroom and discovers we've escaped. I have high hopes that that will unhinge him enough to give the police an added advantage."

"Works for me." Sighing, she leaned her shoulder against the edge of the window. "Chances are good that most of their potential escape routes are covered. I suppose he could bring in a second chopper, but that takes time."

"Very true." Hannah patted Kristy on the shoulder. "As far as you know, are all the latest victims here with us?"

"Yes." The teen smiled slightly. "I can't believe anybody found us. I thought for sure we were goners."

"I know what you mean," Hannah said. "The more I learn about how so many people came together for your rescue, the more impossible it all seems."

"I just wish I could tell my dad," the teen said.

Hannah gestured at Thor. "I'm pretty sure Andy knows by now." A smile blossomed in spite of the still tenuous situation. "My dog is wired."

Hearing that, many of the victims gave a subdued cheer and gathered closer to pet the brave K-9. Hannah warned them off. "Easy. Thor isn't as socialized as most dogs. I haven't had him long enough to be sure he won't get scared and bite."

"This big teddy bear?" Kristy asked, embracing the shepherd with her arms around his shoulders. In response, Thor gave her chin a slurp.

"Maybe I've been underestimating him," Hannah said, amused. "He was picked up as a stray so I can't tell what hang-ups he may have. I do know he's very protective."

"And smart," Lucy added. "We'd never have thought to look behind that heavy cabinet if he hadn't alerted us."

"True." Gazing at the dog with affection, Hannah saw him tilt his head to one side, then rise slowly and take a step toward the closed door to the hallway. "Uh-oh."

"Maybe the cops are already inside and coming for us," Lucy said.

"And maybe not." She pressed her index finger to her lips. "Everybody hush."

In a heartbeat, the only disturbance inside the room was the sound of humans breathing and Thor panting. He put his nose to the carpet and returned to the exit.

Hannah followed. Pressed her ear against the door. Listened. Didn't hear a thing and peered through the tiny peephole.

There was nobody out there. Not a soul. Yet the dog had reacted to something, hadn't he? Her fingers closed around the knob. Did she dare open the door to take a better look?

Before she could decide, Lucy called to her. "Something's up. Something has changed. Look."

Hannah left Thor sniffing at the base of the closed door and returned to the window.

Gram was right. Not only had the string of police cars stopped moving, five of them had gathered directly in front of the hotel with their headlights pointing toward the entrance. Uniformed officers were climbing out and donning riot gear as if they expected to encounter violent resistance. Sadly, they were probably right.

Peeking from his vantage point at the top of the ornate staircase, Rafe could see a lot of what was happening below. He didn't get to watch when Deuce unlocked the ballroom and discovered that the young women were missing but his verbal response was loud enough to echo through the whole hotel.

"Where *are* they?!"

Rafe heard a scuffle, more shouts and curses, then two shots in rapid succession. He hadn't intended for the men he'd captured to be killed, but that couldn't be helped at this point. He'd given them a chance when he'd left them both alive and able-bodied. Momentary guilt assailed him until he reminded himself that he'd acted for the good of innocent victims.

"You and you," Deuce yelled, "go outside and look for them."

"But Boss..."

Rafe expected more shots when whoever Fleming was trying to send hesitated. Because that didn't happen he figured the thugs had obeyed despite their protest.

Bracing himself for others to start up the stairs soon, he leaned a shoulder against a sturdy newel post and aimed low. He didn't have long to wait. Fleming wasn't leading the assault, as Rafe had hoped, but he got off a couple of accurate shots that found their targets and stopped the rest in their tracks.

If there had not been so many armed men milling around the wounded ones on the first floor, Rafe might have gotten off a shot at Fleming, himself.

Someone yelled, "Kill the lights," and in seconds the only illumination of the lobby came from the setting sun and headlights of the patrol cars.

"Smart," Rafe murmured, not at all happy about losing clarity. He could have shot into the shadowy group and would likely have killed or wounded some, but that wasn't the right thing to do. If he intended to fire fatal shots they needed to be aimed and purposeful. Fleming's men might be random killers but they couldn't all be as bad as their leader. Capturing the bulk of them for intense interrogation was the goal of the strike team. It wasn't enough to merely end this facet of the operation here and now. They needed to take down the worldwide network, or at least as much of it as possible.

Shadows moved. Shifted. Rafe peered down. Several armed men had formed a line along the curve of the staircase and were climbing in a crouch.

"Stop. Police," Rafe shouted. "Hands up."

Nobody obeyed. He hadn't expected them to. They did, however, back off and regroup in the lobby. That would do. Anything that delayed the gang's escape gave the multi-agency strike team more time to get into position for a coordinated assault. That was enough. He wasn't hoping for more.

Excitement had caused him to breathe rapidly. Suddenly, his throat itched, then burned. He coughed. His pulse leaped and stayed accelerated far beyond normal, even for a tense situation like this standoff.

Rafe gasped. Was it…? Would he really…? The obvious answer was, *Yes.* Fleming or one of his men had lit the hotel on fire, probably by igniting the spilled gasoline in that janitor's storage room.

"There was no other way to disable those gas bombs," Rafe told himself. There were too many of them to have carried them outside to empty and, given more time, the liquid would have evaporated rendering it useless. When he'd closed the door to keep his countermeasure a secret he'd inadvertently delayed the dispersal of the volatile vapors. Now, anyone inside the hotel was poised to become a victim.

No one stayed at the base of the stairway after the first cry of "Fire" echoed. Climbing away from easy exits would be foolish and these criminals were, for the most part, clever. Fleming was the worst, of course, but he was also teetering on the edge of losing self-control so there was no telling what he might do next.

Only one goal remained for Rafe. He had to find Hannah and the others and rescue them. Without getting himself killed, he added. Acrid smoke stung his eyes, made them water. Every breath, however shallow, made him cough. Fire on the ground floor was sending smoke and sparks up the open stairway as if it were a chimney. With no way to close it off, Rafe was helpless to stop or divert it.

Starting down the nearest hallway he began banging on doors as he passed and shouting "Fire!" at the top of his lungs. The farther he got from the source of the flames the better he could breathe. Smoke was layering on the second floor now, filling the space at the ceiling first, leaving air near the floor more breathable.

If it wouldn't have slowed him down he would have dropped to his knees and crawled. As it was, he bent at the waist and tried to cover his mouth and nose with fabric from his hoodie.

Nobody responded on that floor. Elevators had been out of service all along so he opened a stairway door and ran through, slamming it behind him to slow the rise of the smoke and the spread of the fire.

Arriving on the third floor Rafe secured the stairway door the same way, adding to the fire blocking. As old as the hotel was, hopefully there was not a lot of manmade material in the furnishings because fumes from plastics, etcetera, could be deadly without being concentrated.

A roof access door stood open. He braced, aiming at the space as he passed through to check. There was nobody left up there. At least not that he could see. Which meant the kidnap victims must be already outside on the ground or trapped on the third floor. Like he was.

Rafe turned on his heel, reentered the hotel from the roof access and started down the nearest hallway, hitting doors with the butt of one of the guns and shouting. Half-way down it occurred to him that even if Hannah could hear him she might think it was a trick.

Doubling over coughing, he straightened and yelled, "It's me, Rafe. The hotel's on fire." Every new door he came to got the same message, punctuated by sneezing and coughing and gasping for breath thanks to the doses of smoke he'd taken in below.

His nose was too stuffy to accurately assess the air on that floor, but he imagined there must be enough smoke seeping through for others to smell it. To believe him. To decide to show themselves and come out of wherever they were hiding.

If they stayed hidden for too long they might lose their chance to escape. Even if the old hotel had stood next to a fire station, which it did not, he doubted any efforts would stop the fire from engulfing every floor at this point.

Tears of sorrow mixed with the effects of the smoke and trickled down Rafe's cheeks.

Each step he took was harder, each room he reached seemed farther from the last.

At the far end of the hallway his body gave out. He thudded against the door, hit it with his fist, then dropped to his knees with a feeble, hoarse, "Fire, fire."

TWENTY-THREE

Hannah and Lucy figured out what was wrong when they saw patrol cars gathering and their headlights illuminating the smoke billowing from the first floor. Some of the young women panicked while others were nearly catatonic after their long ordeal and didn't react at all.

"What do you think, Gram?" Hannah asked. "Up or down?"

"Probably up, until we figure out where everybody else is," Lucy said. "See what you can find to use as a weapon."

"I'm way ahead of you," Hannah said. "So is Kristy. She found us a couple of fancy curtain rods with pointy ends."

"You're taking a plastic lance to a gunfight?" Lucy huffed. "I had something a little more lethal in mind."

"Such as?"

"I don't know. I'm just an old lady, past her prime."

"Never," Hannah countered. "You'll never be too old for a fight. I saw you at the church, remember?"

"I do. Seems like that was months ago, not just days. I've aged a lot since."

"We all have," Hannah said. She looked to Kristy. "Look around for something else, something dangerous?"

"A lamp? The rod holding up hangers in the closet? The only other thing is an ironing board."

"Rods are good. Shower rods may be metal. Closet ones, too. And see if you can find the iron that goes with the board. It'll be hard and pointed on one end." Hannah's gaze traveled over the obviously frightened group. "All of you. Look, please. Anything is better than nothing."

Unspoken thoughts enlarged the scenario to include a face-to-face confrontation of her basically defenseless bunch of women against guns. That kind of battle was unwinnable.

So what kind is, at this point? Hannah asked herself, refusing to consider a negative answer.

Thor began to bark at the closed door. Whiffs of smoke rose in faint, twisting columns from beneath, as if someone was out in the hallway smoking a cigarette.

Hannah approached, grabbed his harness with one hand and fisted the base of a table lamp with the other. She called to Kristy. "Open it. And be ready."

"Fast or slow?" the teen asked.

Mouthing *Fast*, Hannah poised to go on the offensive.

Kristy turned the knob. Jerked open the door.

Hannah froze as Rafe McDowell fell face-first at her feet. She dropped to her knees. It was easy to tell he was still breathing because of his gasping and coughing.

She helped him sit up. He looked awful—

and wonderful at the same time. Just having him with her again gave her hope.

"We saw the smoke. How bad is it?"

"Bad," Rafe choked out.

"Can you walk?" He proved the answer by standing. One hand was on the door, one on her shoulder. "Should we head for the roof?"

Rafe nodded. "Can't go down. Too much smoke and fire."

"There are fire hoses in cabinets on the walls in hallways. Can we use those?" Hannah asked. Enough smoke was beginning to reach their floor that she sneezed. Some of the others were already coughing.

"There's no water pressure to fill them," Rafe said. "They're useless."

"Maybe…" Hannah had been planning to rip linen into strips and use that to let everyone safely down from the roof. Now, she had a different idea.

She pushed past Rafe to check the hallway. "One of those hoses is right out there. We can use it like a ladder."

Lucy showed up behind her with the

clothes iron and shouted, "Stand back," as she swung it at the glass cover in front of the fire suppression system.

It shattered. She knocked loose slivers from the frame with the metal iron, then stood back as Rafe pulled on the thick canvas hose. It wasn't long enough to reach very far past the window in the room they'd been hiding in but it looked adequate for a closer one.

Hannah led the way with Thor, taking care to avoid letting him step on broken glass. The guest room next to the fire hose attachment was unlocked, as were they all. She crossed quickly to the window. It wasn't designed to open so she threw a chair at it. The window vibrated but didn't break.

"Bring the iron," she called to her grandmother. "And the rest of you get in here."

Lucy used the cord to swing, whipped the heavy iron around her head like a stone in a sling and let fly at the window. It shattered into a million pieces. Grinning, she turned to Hannah. "David and Goliath."

"Good one." Now that the window was open Hannah could see plenty of activity below. If the siege was going as well as it appeared to be, the Fleming gang had been overcome.

She turned to the kidnap victims. "We're going to drop this hose out the window. You're all young and strong so you should be able to slide down. Hook one arm around it if you don't think you can hang onto the canvas covering well enough."

"I'm scared of heights," one of the girls said.

"Me, too," another echoed.

"Everybody join hands," Hannah ordered, reaching for the closest person and finding it was Rafe. She clasped his fingers tightly and felt an immediate surge of determination and strength. "We're going to pray, then we'll do this. Understand?"

Nodding, the others followed her instructions. She bowed. "Thank You, Father, for showing us a way out. Help us to complete Your plans for our rescue. Amen."

That was all that needed to be said, she

decided. The asking was one step. Following through was another.

Hannah took Thor to the window, watched as Rafe and Kristy dropped the hose its full length, then backed away. She held out a hand. "Okay. Who's first?"

It had immediately occurred to her that Thor would be unable to descend the way the humans did. She vowed to get him out of the burning building one way or another, even if it meant staying with him until a fire truck with a ladder eventually arrived. She refused to entertain the notion that that might happen too late for both her and her beloved dog.

The vibration of his cell phone caught Rafe's attention. He stepped away from the window where he, Lucy and Hannah had been helping a young women over the sill and out the window. Three of them had already reached the ground and been scooped up by troopers.

"Hello."

"Status?" his superintendent asked, shouting over the background noise.

"We're on the third floor. All the victims we knew about are present, including Kristy Fellows. We've rigged a line from a window to the ground and so far it's working."

"How many more do you have?"

Rafe did a quick count. "Looks like about eighteen, not including me, Hannah Lassiter or her grandmother."

"All right. Make it fast. Fire units are still twenty to thirty minutes out. You need to evacuate."

"Copy," Rafe said. His gaze met Hannah's and lingered. "Everybody goes out the window."

"I'm not leaving Thor."

"I figured that's what you'd say. Lucy and I can handle this. You go find something to make a sling for him and I'll take him down with me."

"That's too dangerous."

"For me or for the dog?" Rafe asked, slightly perturbed.

"For both of you," Hannah answered.

He didn't like seeing tears filling her eyes. She must not give up. Not now. Not when they were so close to their goal.

"My jacket was okay for the short drop back at your house. I don't think it's secure enough for the trip down the hose. You need to rig something that fits my shoulders and attaches to his harness."

In obvious agreement, Lucy left the window with Hannah and the dog. Rafe's fondest hope was that the older woman's arms were also strong enough to keep her from falling when she took her turn to shinny down the fire hose. If it had been filled with water it would have been about two inches in diameter. Flat, it was harder to grasp securely. Not impossible, just more difficult.

He lost count of how many victims he had assisted. Turning to welcome the next he saw only Hannah, Lucy and Thor. "Ready?"

"Gram will go next," Hannah said, displaying a ripped, knotted sheet. "We've tied these strips together with a loop on one end. She'll wear it as a safety harness, then we'll pull it back up and tie a figure eight for your shoulders and fasten Thor's harness to it."

Rafe gestured to her. "Okay. You next."

"No." Hannah was shaking her head vigorously. She coughed. "I'm last."

"Unacceptable," Rafe countered.

"I have to be here to help you rig the dog for transport. He trusts me."

"He trusts me, too."

"Enough to let you manhandle him and sling him across your back? Are you sure?" She paused for a moment. "I'm the dog expert. You need to listen to me."

As much as he disliked the idea, he knew she was right. "Okay. Lucy next, then me and the dog. But I expect to see you right behind me. Promise?"

She raised a hand, palm toward him as if taking an oath. "Promise."

Lucy slipped a loop of torn sheet over her shoulders and under her arms, wincing from the pain in her ribs, then put a leg out the window. Assisting her, Rafe felt her trembling yet she showed no more outward signs of discomfort other than gritted teeth and a deep scowl. Hannah's grandma was quite extraordinary.

That thought almost made Rafe smile. Coughing hid his temporary amusement. The smoke was getting thicker, more acrid, partly because the fire below was building and partly because they had been unable to shut the door with the hose passing through its opening.

Lucy shouted and waved once her feet touched ground. Rafe hauled the sheet back up, hand over hand. Hannah was waiting to tie more knots and form a figure eight like a backpack for him to carry Thor. She explained as she prepared to tie a portion of the sheet line to the dog's harness.

"I think that will work," Rafe said, intending to encourage her.

"It had better. Sit down on the floor so I can get him closer to your back. I'll lift him when you stand up and help you through the window."

That gave Rafe pause. "Are you sure we'll fit?" Lack of an answer was his answer. She didn't know. Neither did he. They'd have to try it to find out.

Supporting Thor and speaking gently to calm him, Hannah finished tying the knots. "Okay, Rafe, on your feet. I'll lift Thor as much as I can before I have to let go. You're bound to be off balance so plan for it."

"Gotcha." The weight of the dog would have been more of a problem if he'd tried to walk very far carrying him. As it was, the few steps to the window were manageable. He bent at the waist, still coughing some, and sat on the sill.

"Try to hold him up while I get both legs out and around the hose," Rafe said. "I'll tell you when to let go."

"Okay."

He could see her teeth clenching, a grimace on her face as she struggled to help him balance the heavy dog. Turning, he let himself down until he was hanging on the hose, alone.

"I'll keep hold of the extra sheet for as

long as I can, just like we did with Gram. It might help."

"Okay, as long as you don't stop my descent," Rafe warned. "It may be a little fast." Hannah was letting the ripped fabric slip through her fingers as he pushed off and started down.

The trip took every spare ounce of his strength. When he landed there were men waiting to relieve him of his canine burden and congratulate him on the success of the mass escape.

Rafe looked up expecting to see Hannah traveling down, herself. Instead, she was leaning out the window, watching him. He gave her a thumbs-up sign and waved. "Come on."

Suddenly, her head and shoulders disappeared. Rafe held his breath waiting for her to stick a foot out and swing around to grasp the hose.

She did not.

TWENTY-FOUR

Hannah whirled. A shadowy figure appeared in the doorway behind her. For an instant she wondered if one of the troopers or government agents had come to rescue her. Then she realized who it actually was.

She backed up as far as she could. Her hips hit the window sill and she froze.

Deuce Fleming was coughing worse than Rafe had been so it took him a few seconds to speak. "Last man standing wins."

Although Hannah wanted to match wits with him and stall the inevitable, astonishment kept her quiet. This was not supposed to end this way. The good guys were supposed to win. And they had for the most part. Only one person was left to face this evil man because the rest of his victims had escaped and there was nothing he could do about it.

Except kill me, she added, wondering if it was actually God's will that her earthly life end then and there.

"Please, no, Lord," she whispered. "I don't want to die. Not now. Not like this. I haven't even had a chance to tell Rafe how much he means to me."

A massive coughing fit doubled Fleming over and he lowered the gun.

That was all Hannah needed. She threw one leg through the open window and grabbed for the hose. It slipped out of her grasp. Her second leg bent at the knee to keep her from falling, but it also kept her within range of her worst enemy.

Trying again she looped her whole arm around the hose and let herself drop outside. Both arms and legs circled the hose, slowing her descent as the rough canvas scraped off skin. Adjusting her hold she looked up. Fleming was leaning out the window and pointing his gun down at her. There was no way to duck. No way to dodge. Even if she let go and fell she'd probably die when she hit the ground so she just hung on and kept sliding.

Ten feet from the bottom she heard and saw an explosion. A ball of fire blossomed out the third floor window and the hose went slack, dropping her into Rafe's waiting embrace.

Flabbergasted, Hannah wrapped her arms around his neck as he carried her toward a waiting ambulance. Thor galloped along at his feet, barking as if they were playing a wonderful game.

The rumble of Rafe's voice was drowned out by the pounding beats of her heart and repeated explosions within the old hotel. Hannah didn't care what had blown up or why. She was simply overcome by the timing and the way God had implemented her rescue—with the use of her favorite state trooper, of course.

Clinging tightly, Hannah closed her eyes and buried her face against his smoky shoulder, hardly able to process what had just happened. None of her efforts should have been enough, yet they were. Imagine, a powerful explosion at just the right moment and this amazing man waiting below and risking his life to stay close enough to catch her.

He didn't loosen his hold and set her on her feet until they were back behind the carriage house where several ambulances waited next to the command post van. Then, he set her away, keeping hold of her shoulders.

"What do you think?" he asked, looking worried.

"About what?"

"About what I just told you."

Befuddled, Hannah kept gazing at him and cupped one of his cheeks gently. "I can hardly hear you, even now," she said. "The explosion hurt my ears."

"You're going to make me say it again, aren't you?"

Continuing to caress his beard-stubbled cheek, she smiled up at him. "If it was something good, yes."

He leaned closer to place a kiss on her smoky forehead. "I said I love you."

Hearing her own thoughts echoed was both wonderful and terrifying. "I—I was afraid of that."

"Why?"

Honesty was clearly called for and she chose her words carefully. "The only thing you and I have in common is this terrible situation. Now that it's over, what connects us?"

"I guess we'll have to get to know each other better and find out, won't we?"

"If that's what you want."

"What do you want?" Rafe asked, pulling her so close his lips brushed her temple.

Hannah was smiling when she said, "You. Whoever you are."

EPILOGUE

Posing in front of a full length mirror, Hannah smiled at her grandmother's reflection behind her. "I can't believe this is happening, can you?"

"As a matter of fact, I can." Eyes twinkling Lucy smoothed the flowing skirt of her Matron of Honor dress. "What I can't believe is that you chose this smoky blue color. It matches my eyes perfectly."

"It's a good thing Gavin and I waited a couple of months after we decided to get married or you might have had circles under your eyes to match, too." Hannah embraced her. "I'm so thankful you weren't hurt worse in that crash."

"Don't hug me too tightly, okay? I'm still sore in places."

"You were amazing, Gram."

"Not half as amazing as your future husband was—and is." She chuckled under her breath. "I don't know if I'll ever get over wanting to call him Rafe."

"I know. But I like his real name, too. In a couple of hours I'll be Mrs. Gavin Arthur."

"So you will." Lucy sighed. "It takes me back, seeing you in my old wedding dress. I can't believe you wanted to wear it."

"Don't be silly. I love vintage." Running her hands over the sleek curves of the ivory colored satin, she gave a little kick to ripple the wider, fluted hem, then picked up a crown of real flowers.

"You're a beautiful bride, Hannah. I'm just surprised you didn't want a more fashionable dress."

"A more *normal* one, you mean?" She laughed. "Gavin asked me the same thing. He even offered to pay for it."

"Really? What did you tell him?"

"I reminded him that there had never been anything very normal about me or my family and suggest he'd better get used to it."

"Did he laugh?" Lucy asked with a smile.

Hannah felt her cheeks flush and saw them reddening in the mirror. "Actually," she said, pausing briefly for a sigh, "he picked me up, swung me around and kissed me breathless."

"I knew he was a keeper," Lucy said, patting her own pink cheeks with a lace handkerchief as if perspiring.

Hannah reached for her grandmother's hands and clasped them, hanky and all. "Are you sure you won't change your mind and move in with us after we come back from our honeymoon? We have plenty of room." It touched her to see happy tears welling in the older woman's eyes and her own began to fill as well.

"I'm sure."

"But what will you do with yourself when you don't have me to look after and fuss over?"

"I'll have Thor for company while you're gone. After that, I'll adjust." Lucy stood tall with her chin jutting proudly. "I was saving this for a surprise but now is as good a time as any, I guess. I'm going back to work."

"Not as a…"

"Don't be silly. Of course not." A grin split her face and tiny lines accented the corners of her eyes before she said, "I'll be joining a senior citizens group that tours all over the world." She paused, winked and added, "What could be more innocent than a dozen or so old retired folks just hanging around touristy hot spots, listening to local gossip and taking it easy?"

"A dozen plain citizens or a dozen former spies?"

Pulling away, Lucy arched an eyebrow. "You just take care of your dog and your new husband, honey. I'll send you postcards from all the exotic places I go."

"And you'll phone me at least once a week," Hannah added. "Promise?"

"I do," Lucy said before giggling. "Hey, that's supposed to be your line."

A sharp knock on the door caught Hannah's attention. Smiling at Gram's silly joke she opened it. Her other bridesmaid, Kristy

Fellows, was acting breathless. "Are you ready?"

"Very."

"Are you sure you want Lucy to give you away? My dad said he could do that and still be the best man."

"I'm positive. Gram raised me. She should be the one to walk me down the aisle."

Accepting the larger of two bouquets from Lucy, Hannah followed Kristy into the church foyer.

Ushers opened double doors for Kristy to precede them. Lucy took Hannah's arm. They stepped forward together.

Hannah realized that if her grandmother had not been there to provide support she might have faltered the moment she laid eyes on her beloved. Gavin was waiting at the altar, just as he had waited at the end of that fire hose to save her life—a life she was now going to share with him.

Blinking, she willed away her happy tears and took the first steps into her future.

* * * * *

Dear Reader,

First, let me assure you that I invented both Lyell Prison and the abandoned hotel on Gabaret. Sometimes it's necessary to bend the truth a bit and, after all, this is a work of fiction.

The spiritual truths in this book, however, reflect my personal beliefs and the way I try to handle the difficulties life throws at me by leaning on my faith. It is my pleasure to have written over seventy-five stories for Love Inspired since the imprint began back in 1997, and each one has blessed me. Each one has also taught me things as I puzzled out life and relied on faith with my characters.

It's a journey I have been thrilled to share with all my readers. God is in the details, as always.

Many Blessings,
Valerie Hansen